Lily
and the NIGHT
CREATURES

*For Ben, who made not only
this book better.*
—N. L.

*For Stephen Alexander
(Sprout), who touched hearts.*
—E. G.

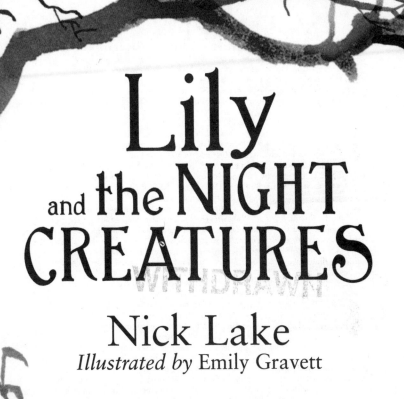

Lily
and the NIGHT
CREATURES

Nick Lake
Illustrated by Emily Gravett

Simon & Schuster Books for Young Readers
New York • London • Toronto • Sydney • New Delhi

SIMON & SCHUSTER BOOKS FOR YOUNG READERS
An imprint of Simon & Schuster Children's Publishing Division
1230 Avenue of the Americas, New York, New York 10020

For information about special discounts for bulk purchases, please contact Simon & Schuster Special Sales at 1-866-506-1949 or business@simonandschuster.com.
The Simon & Schuster Speakers Bureau can bring authors to your live event. For more information or to book an event, contact the Simon & Schuster Speakers Bureau at 1-866-248-3049 or visit our website at www.simonspeakers.com.
Also available in a Simon & Schuster Books for Young Readers paperback edition
The text for this book was set in Sabon.
Manufactured in the United States of America
0722 FFG
First US Edition
2 4 6 8 10 9 7 5 3 1

Library of Congress Cataloging-in-Publication Data
Names: Lake, Nick, author.
Title: Lily and the night creatures / Nick Lake.
Description: First US edition. | New York : Simon & Schuster Books for Young Readers, [2021] | Audience: Ages 8-12. | Audience: Grades 4-6. | Summary: Lily is chronically ill, but while her parents are welcoming a new baby she sneaks home from her grandmother's house and, aided by animal friends, combats the demons who have moved in.
Identifiers: LCCN 2020050963 (print) | LCCN 2020050964 (ebook) | ISBN 9781534494619 (hardcover) | ISBN 9781534494626 (paperback) ISBN 9781534494633 (ebook)
Subjects: CYAC: Adventure and adventurers—Fiction. | Doppelgängers—Fiction. | Animals—Fiction. | Chronic diseases—Fiction. | Family life—Fiction. | Fantasy.
Classification: LCC PZ7.L15857 Lil 2021 (print) | LCC PZ7.L15857 (ebook) | DDC [Fic]—dc23
LC record available at https://lccn.loc.gov/2020050963
LC ebook record available at https://lccn.loc.gov/2020050964

"*The Wizard of Oz* is ending.
We know this because we can hear Judy Garland,
reciting the same five words over and over in a soft, yearning
voice, saying—well, you know what she
is saying. They are only the loveliest five words
ever said in all of film."

Joe Hill, "20th Century Ghost"

BEFORE THE BEGINNING

In the garden of the house a mole was talking to a crow. The sun was setting—that was the time of day, but it was also the reason the animals were visible at all. In the daytime they could not be seen, unless they wanted to be.

"Do you think she will be here soon?" said the mole. "The girl?"

"I don't know," said the crow, hopping from one foot to the other. "Why should I?"

"I tunnel in darkness," said the mole. "You're clever. You soar. In the air."

"I'm clever too!" said a mouse. He was leaning against the severed trunk of a tree.

"No, you're not," said the mole.

"True," said the mouse, not very sadly. "But I'm willing."

"We'll all have to be willing, if the girl is going to win," said the crow.

There was a long pause then. The house was a looming presence in front of them, its edges becoming less definite as the light faded from the sky. The mole sniffed the air. She smelled . . . something that could not be put into words. A certain slackness in the evening, but a dangerous one. Something laid out as if loose, on the framework of the world, that might at any moment be pulled taut.

"Goodness, we're all very serious, aren't we?" said the mouse. "Shall I sing a song?"

"Only if you want me to eat you," said a snake who had slithered up to join them. "Don't think I won't."

"Fine," said the mouse with a *humph*.

They watched the house.

"She won't win if she doesn't come," said the mouse eventually. "She will come, won't she?"

"She'll come," said the mole. "I can smell it."

"Well, there we have it," said the crow. "Mole's nose has spoken."

"It was my mouth actua—Oh."

The crow had given Mole a withering glance. "Now hush," he said, folding his wings. "We don't want them to hear us."

The animals fell silent and watched the house. It was empty, but it was quick—in the old sense of the word, and it was the old senses the animals cared about most. Quivering with life.

A shadow moved past a window, though there was no light to explain it.

The animals shivered—even the snake, who was cold-blooded, and the mole, who couldn't see.

They waited.

The house didn't want her; Lily could see that right away.

It was her house, but it was dark, no lights on, the windows square black holes in the wall. Like someone had put out its eyes. Even the streetlight just at the end of the road had blown. The nearest light came from the pub down the lane, and that wasn't close. The Sherborne Arms. Sometimes at night drunk people rolled bottles out into the road, to burst car tires. The housing committee had been round.

Lily was stubborn, though. She wasn't going to let the house scare her.

"I just need to go in for a minute," Granny Squeak said from the driver's seat of the car. Lily called her Granny

Squeak because when Lily had been little, her granny would always squeak with excitement when she saw her. Now she was more liable to sigh or get wet around the eyes.

"Okay," said Lily, unclicking her seat belt. She wanted to be at home, in her kitchen, in her room: it was what had gotten her through the day. She wanted Willo, even though she was too old for him, really.

"Oh, no, sweetie," said Granny. "You stay here and rest. I'll only be a minute. Your mum's left instructions."

"Okay," said Lily again. "Could you get me Willo?"

It was the kind of thing she would never have admitted to Scarlett and Summer, back when they were still friends. That she still slept with him, a soft toy. Of course, they weren't her friends anymore anyway. People tended to draw away from her now, like what she had might be catching.

But Granny was already out of the door, then shutting it with a heavy *clunk*. She left the engine running. It was springtime but still chilly.

Leaning back into the passenger's seat, Lily closed her eyes. She had just left the hospital and her mum had gone into it, with her dad. To have The Baby. Lily didn't actually know if it was the same hospital; she didn't know anything apart from what her grandmother had told her when she picked her up this morning. That The Baby was coming. That Lily was going to stay with her for a few days. That Granny Squeak was going to look after her, and they could even stay up to watch *EastEnders*.

Big whoop, Lily wanted to say to that.

Her arm was still sore, from the drip. When she went there, to the hospital, they took the liquid out of her veins and cleaned it and did other things to it that Lily didn't understand, then they put it back in. Like they were sucking her out and filling her with a new person, and only the outline of her stayed the same. She didn't like that idea.

And it took all day, with Granny Squeak sitting there reading her *People's Friend* magazine and Lily listening to music and scrolling through TikTok. Usually it was her parents who took her, and it should have been nice getting to spend the day with Granny Squeak instead, but Lily was too distracted by everything.

At the end of today's session the doctor, who had a mustache like a walrus, had come up to her with another needle. Lily hated needles. Especially injections, which she knew perfectly well didn't make sense, because she'd already sort of had a needle in her hand all day, under a bandage, with a tube coming out of it. But that was different. That wasn't a sharp, thin thing going into your muscle.

"Iron," he'd explained. "Your levels get low otherwise; you don't make enough of it."

"I'm fine with that," she'd said. "Can't I just eat some nails or something?"

"Ha ha," he'd said. Actually said. Not laughter. "You won't be fine if you eat nails, trust me."

So she'd closed her eyes and cried a bit, which she was embarrassed about, and he'd done the injection.

She'd made her mum cry the other day, and that was worse.

"We thought we'd talk about names, for the baby," her mum had said. Dad was holding her hand, smiling.

"I don't want to," Lily had replied.

"That's okay. We don't have to decide now."

"I don't want to, ever. I don't want The Baby. I don't want you to be big and fat and round, and I don't want this." She'd pushed her pills and water away from her, across the oak table in the new kitchen that was traced all over with thin lines and swirls of color, from her pens when she was younger. "I want to go back. To how everything used to be."

That was when her mum had cried.

The door of the car swung open with a rush of cool air,

scented with a bonfire somewhere. Granny Squeak hefted a big duffel bag into the back seat, along with a couple of shopping bags, then climbed in behind the wheel.

"Your mum left a note on the table," she said. "Phone number of the hospital, that sort of thing. And a list of everything you'd need, in case they have to stay in for a few days. Clothes, frozen meals. Your meds. But you might have to help with all that!" she added, in what was clearly supposed to be a cheerful tone. "I'm no good with timings."

She started the engine and pulled away.

"Sure," said Lily, without really meaning it. "Did you get Willo?"

"Oh!" said Granny Squeak. "Was he on the list? Sorry. I must have missed that. Oh well, too late now." She shifted into fourth gear.

"No," said Lily. "I asked as you were—"

She stopped. There was no point. Willo was her whale: Lily had slept with him most nights of her life and wasn't sure she could sleep without him. He was from IKEA, which wasn't important, but she'd gotten him when she was two, the very first toy she'd ever chosen herself, and that *was* important.

Lily *needed* Willo, and Willo wasn't there.

But that was okay. Because Lily had no intention of being shunted aside, of being sent away from home, anyway. Everyone else thought they knew best—but it was her home too. Her home *first*.

2

They drove to Granny's house. It wasn't far—on the edge of the same village. Lily and her mum and dad moved there from London partly because of that. When Lily was little and better.

For dinner Granny made what she thought, for some reason lost to Lily's memory, was Lily's favorite dish, but which Lily actually hated. Potatoes and cream and spinach and lots of black pepper. Granny didn't believe in using salt in her cooking, which was why most of her cooking wasn't very nice to eat, in Lily's opinion.

After supper Granny said, "You must be tired."

"What if I'm not?" said Lily.

Granny blinked. She often looked, these days, like she wasn't sure who Lily was. Like when they put Lily's blood through those machines, they really did make her into a different person.

"Never mind," said Lily after a moment of silence.

They went upstairs. Lily always slept in the guest bedroom opposite Granny's room—there was a TV on a stand in the corner she didn't know how to turn on, and every surface was covered with fabric that had been embroidered, knitted, or crocheted. The bed was very soft, though, and comfortable. It was like being the princess from *The Princess and the Pea*, only without the pea.

Lily got into her pajamas, which Granny had brought, and then snuggled under the covers. Granny said good night and kissed her on the forehead, which was nice, actually, and made Lily feel a bit guilty over what she was about to do. At the same time Lily was thinking about sickness, and what came after, which was not so nice. She knew Granny always prayed by her bed every night. Like a picture from an old storybook.

"Granny Squeak," she said, "do you believe in heaven?"

"Yes and no," said Granny Squeak.

Lily was surprised by this. "Really?"

"Well," said her granny, pausing at the door. "When people talk about heaven, they usually mean something far away, in the sky, that comes after you . . . um . . . pass on. But I don't think heaven is like that. I think it's low down—and everywhere, even when you're still here. You only have to decide to see it."

"Oh," said Lily. She half smiled. Yes. She could imagine that. It was a nice idea, anyway.

"Night, love," said her granny.

"Night," said Lily.

She switched off her bedside lamp, making the room disappear in an instant, and listened to Granny Squeak's soft, slippered footsteps crossing the corridor. She knew Granny would read before going to sleep. Thrillers. Large print. Lily lay there, her eyes wide open, and thought about heaven. For her, if heaven was down here and not up in the sky, it would be the time before. Before she got ill. Before The Baby came into her mum's tummy and their lives.

Before: Her mum crouching down, to her level, which was never a good sign, and taking a long strip of glossy photo film from her handbag. A vague outline of a baby, white against black, its hand raised. Her dad's voice: "We wanted to wait, until the anatomy scan, because . . . In case something went wrong."

In case something was wrong like it's wrong with me, Lily had thought.

So, yes, she'd rewind—zip; her life flashing past backward, right back to before she got sick, before there was a fuzzy, monochrome baby in her mum's stomach.

But Lily couldn't go back in time, no matter what Granny Squeak said about deciding what heaven was.

She couldn't go back to how everything used to be—but she *could* go back to her house, tonight, and find that note from her mum. Granny Squeak didn't seem to have it—Lily had looked in her bag when she was in the bathroom Which meant it was probably still at Lily's house.

Even if it was all dark and unwelcoming outside, she just needed to get to the house, find out what hospital her parents had gone to, and follow them. In a taxi? Yes, maybe in a taxi. Or something. She'd sort that out when she came to it.

She wasn't going to stay at Granny Squeak's while her mum and dad had The Baby without her, like she was some sort of afterthought; she wasn't about to be replaced that easily. If they were going to ruin everything, she wanted to at least be there. Otherwise it, The Baby, would have a head start.

Lily should be there—and was *going* to be there—to remind her parents that they already had her, that she was first, and that even though she was faulty, was damaged, they couldn't just forget about her.

Yes, as soon as Granny Squeak was asleep, Lily was going to run away from her house and go home.

3

Running away from Granny's house: that bit was easy.

Going home?

Not so much, it turned out.

Lily waited until her granny was asleep—deep, rhythmical snoring coming from the room across the hallway, the sliver of light below the door gone to blackness—and then she crept along the landing toward the stairs. It helped that Granny Squeak had carpet everywhere, in an old-fashioned fleur-de-lis pattern.

"Lily carpet for my Lily girl," Granny would say. "Always makes me think of you."

Lily wasn't wild about being associated with flooring, but she didn't say so.

For now, though, the thick carpet was useful in muffling sound. Lily tiptoed down the stairs, past the rails for the stairlift that her granddad had used when he was alive and that Granny Squeak hadn't gotten around to taking out yet, then into the short hallway.

She didn't even try the front door—she knew it would creak too much. She went straight through the linoleum-floored kitchen to the back door, which had a little porch attached to it, and out into the garden. The dark had turned trees and buildings into vague shapes, transformed ghosts of themselves. Lily shivered and took a strengthening breath before she stepped out.

The garden backed onto the yard of the church where Lily had been christened, where they still went for midnight mass on Christmas Eve.

"A bit High Church for me," Granny once said. Lily didn't know what that meant, but she had a feeling she disagreed. She liked the candles and the incense. They felt like spells.

From the back porch of Granny's house, Lily could even see her own tree, which her parents had planted in the church-yard when she was born. It was a May tree, because she'd been born in May. A short, stunted thing, bent by the wind.

"Roots in the earth, branches in heaven"—that was

what Dad always said. Though Granny was right that heaven was pretty low down, if the warped branches of the May tree were anything to go by.

"You should have planted a lily," Lily had said recently.
"Lilies don't live very long," her father had said.
Lily: "Well, me neither, if I'm not lucky."

That was another time she had made her
mother cry.

Now Lily climbed over the low wall of the
garden and into Church Lane, then followed it
to the green. She went over the little wooden
footbridge by the weeping willow, its branches
stirring in the breeze, as if reaching out to stroke
her. She worried that her footsteps even *sounded*
nervous. Staccato and faltering. And then she went
round the long, sweeping road that cut through the back of
the village, until she reached her own lane.

Only . . . it didn't seem like hers now. Trees cast tall,
skinny shadows, like fingers, across the road. The streetlight
was still out. Clouds covered the sky, and there was only a
thin sliver of moon anyway, a little shining nick opened by
a blade in the darkness. The lights of the house at the end of
the lane remained off.

Lily shivered, hugging her loose hoodie around her. All
her clothes were loose these days.

She felt more afraid than she would like; it clung to her
like a too-tight coat. She tried to shrug it off. This was *her*
house.

She took a step forward. From her pocket, she grabbed

her key, then walked up the little path to the front door. On her left was a construction dumpster, full of planks of wood and broken bits of plaster. The upstairs was still being remodeled; the workers hadn't finished it in time for The Baby. Running down to the dumpster, from scaffolding attached to the top floor, was a long tube made of plastic segments pushed into one another, like a slide at a water park. The builders used it to slide junk down to the dumpster.

Lily stopped. Just for a moment she thought she'd seen movement, behind the curtains. A twitch. A swish.

The bunch of keys shook, very lightly, in her hand. A high metal sound.

No. There was no one. Silly. The house was empty.

It was an old, old door, with four little windowpanes at the top, divided by lead.

She lifted the key and put it into the lock. There were actually two locks on the door—the lower one was ancient, with a worn-smooth, knob-shaped handle of brass that glinted even in the dark, and on both sides an old-fashioned hole, the classic keyhole shape. But no one had ever found the key, and the lock was unlocked anyway, its tongue held inside the old iron body that housed it, so she and her parents only used the lower lock.

She was just turning the key when the door opened, inward, and she nearly fell inside.

Her mother stood there, in the hallway, which had a new and shiny parquet floor. They'd been doing lots of renovating, extending the house, getting it ready for The Baby . . .

Which was in her mother's arms. A baby, looking at Lily with eyes that seemed much too big for its head. Or was it looking? Its eyes were oddly still and black.

The hall was dark. The lamp on the wall by the key cupboard was not lit; none of the lights were on.

"Who's that?" called her dad, from the living room, it sounded like.

"I don't know," Lily's mother called back. Then she turned to Lily. Her eyes were black too, like the baby's. A dull black. They were not the eyes of Lily's mum. "Hello," she said. "Who are you? Can I help you?"

Lily took a step back. She had to make an effort to send warmth into her vocal cords, to unfreeze them so that she could speak. "It's me. Lily," she said. "I live here."

Her mother laughed a hollow laugh that was not her real laugh. "Oh, of course," she said. "You're the daughter. But, no, you don't live here anymore."

And she shut the door.

4

For a long moment Lily just stood there, as if she and her birth tree had swapped places, as if she had put down roots. She imagined the tree hoisting up its branches and setting off from the graveyard, stalking down the road, dripping earth.

She stumbled backward. Tears were welling up in her eyes, like they had when she'd left the house last time, for the hospital, only worse, because now she wasn't just angry, she was scared.

She blinked furiously. What?

What?

Then the last thing she had said to her parents that morning came back to her. "It's my due date, Lils," her mum had said, speaking softly, to explain why she couldn't go with her.

"That doesn't mean anything, does it?" Lily had said.

"Well . . . there are some signs. It could be Braxton Hicks," her mum had added hurriedly. "But it could be today. You might be meeting the baby soon."

Lily had been getting ready for her day of appointments, downloading an album and putting on her coat. She couldn't bear the tentative half smile on her mum's face. "Whatever," she'd said. "I might just not come home. I don't want to see The Baby. Actually, I don't want to see you or Dad. I don't want to see you ever again."

Then she'd walked out of the door, to where Granny was waiting in the car.

She blinked again as she stood in front of the shut door of the dark house. Had she done this? Had she cast some kind of spell with her words?

For a moment she considered going back to Granny Squeak's house—to its warmth and deep carpets. But Granny would just say she was overtired; Lily could almost hear the kind words she would use.

And, anyway, Lily was still stubborn, and she wasn't going to let whatever was happening stop her from getting into her own home. Wasn't going to let whatever had replaced her mum lock her out. Not without doing some investigating at least.

Lily cut across the field next to her house and went round to the back garden, past the shed where the lawn mower and her bike were kept, along with a load of spiderwebs. Past the remains of the little snowman she'd made that Christmas. Not snow—that had melted long ago. But what with her mother's condition, no one had gotten around to bringing in the scarf, which lay curled up on the grass like a sad snake's shed skin, or the moldy carrot, or the two pieces of coal that had been the eyes. She stepped past it all and onto the wide part of the lawn.

The garden had changed a lot in the last few months: the old cottage they'd moved into had been shaped like the letter *L*, with a patio. Now the patio was gone and the open part of the *L* had been filled in with a shiny new kitchen extension, bifold glass doors at the end. There had been an apple tree, a cherry tree, and several bushes, including an old and wiry blackberry plant. Those were gone too, leaving only a flat expanse of lawn.

So flat, in fact, that it was a surprise when Lily tripped over something as she walked through the garden and fell facedown on the lawn, smushing dew-wet grass into her nose and mouth.

"Ugh," she said, spitting out earth.

She stood and examined what had caught her foot, picking it up: an ancient horseshoe, iron and rusted. She recognized the thing. It had hung above their old back door, before their old back door became just an opening into the new kitchen.

"That should go back up, really."

Lily whirled, looking for the source of the voice.

"Down here."

She looked down. A mole was standing at her feet. Or not standing. Could something that already had four legs stand? It was *there*, anyway, on its four paws. Did moles have paws? Lily was a little afraid that she was losing her mind. Or that she had fallen asleep in the embroidered bed at Granny's and this was a dream. In dreams, though, grass did not tend to be so wet that it squelched under your feet.

"Did you . . . did you speak?" she asked.

"Oh, yes," said the mole. "I'd have written a letter, but that wouldn't have been very efficient, what with you standing right above me."

Lily opened her mouth, then closed it again.

"Mole's right, though," said someone else. A higher voice, croaky. "The horseshoe belongs where it belongs, and where it belongs is on the back of the house." The voice was coming from above and to the right—Lily turned her head to see a large black crow sitting on the shed at the side of the lawn.

"Hello," it said.

5

U m. Hello," said Lily to the crow. "Am I . . . Am I dreaming?"

The crow ruffled its feathers. "Dreaming, it says!" Lily did not especially appreciate being called an "it," by a crow of all things, but she appreciated what happened next even less.

Taking off from the shed, the crow flew toward her, banked upward in the air, rattled over her head with a close, rushing rustle of wings, and dropped something wet on her hair, with a splat.

Lily raised her hand instinctively to touch her head, then thought better of it. The crow returned to the shed and sat, preening and looking very pleased with itself.

"I just did a fat dropping on your head," said the crow. "Would that happen in a dream?"

Lily considered this. "Probably, yes."

"Hmm. Perhaps it was a bad example."

"Also quite disgusting," said Lily. Her voice sounded far away and hollow.

"Well, sorry about that. We're quite clean, if that helps. Not like pigeons. You could use Mole to wipe it off?"

"She couldn't," said the mole.

Lily sighed. Even if this was a dream—which seemed horribly unlikely—that didn't change the fact that she had bird poo in her hair. She put down the horseshoe and went over to some tins of paint near the dark glass of the extension. The whole house was dark, from this side too. Nothing moved inside. Yet she crouched low as she picked up a rag that had been left on one of the tins by the decorators, lest anything inside the house should see her.

Wincing, she rubbed at her head until it felt clean. Then she walked back up the garden. The mole and the crow were still there, looking at her with eyes that were not so much beady as jewel-like, glittering in the dark. Almost as if they were expecting something from her. Like they had been waiting for her.

"The mole's name is, um, just Mole?" she asked.

"What else would it be?" said Mole. "Names are a human thing."

Lily inclined her head to one side. "Dolphins have names," she said. "Mrs. Beaney said so, at school. Like, little songs and clicks and whatever that belong only to that dolphin. They learn them quite young. And—" But she stopped, realizing that shock was making her babble.

"They'd need them," said the crow. "I mean, I'd want a name if I were a dolphin. They all look the same. As it is, I am just Crow."

"Well . . . ," said Lily.

"Well, what?"

"Crows . . . sort of . . . all look the same too."

The crow ruffled its feathers indignantly. "How dare you? I'll have you know I am a very handsome crow."

"Ooooh. Is he?" said Mole. "I can't see very well. It's the living underground."

"I don't know!" said Lily. Had one of her injections done something to her mind? "He's a crow!"

"Harrumph," said Crow, tucking his head under his wing.

"You've offended him now," said Mole. "They're touchy, crows."

Lily put her head in her hands. "What are you *doing* here?" she said. "Why are you *talking*? What do you *want*?"

"We don't *want* anything," said Crow, untucking. "I myself rarely want things. Apart from cherries, maybe. It's a shame your parents chopped down the cherry tree. Lovely cherries, those. Mole, I suppose, wants worms. It's all she eats and—"

"Hush," said Mole indulgently. "We're here because you need us," she added to Lily, because apparently she was a she. As it were.

"Need you?"

"To help you get back into your house. To evict the replacements."

"The replacements . . . ?"

"The things in the house that look like your parents."

"Oh," said Lily, thinking of her mother, with her flat black eyes.

"That's why we're here," said the mole.

"Right," said Lily. Everything seemed to have gone very gloopy, as if the air had been changed to something else, like treacle. "So . . . I'm supposed to get into my house and get rid of those . . . things . . . that look like my parents, and I'm going to be helped by . . . a mole. And a crow?"

"Oh, no," said the crow.

"No?" A flush of relief spread through Lily's midsection, a true thing she could feel, warm and liquid, true as her own blood. This wasn't real. Things were going to start making sense again.

"Well, yes. But not *just* us. Mouse is going to help too." The crow bent his head, eyeing Lily's feet. Lily looked down.

A little gray mouse was there, holding what looked like a needle as if it were a sword.

"I'm small, but I'm mighty," said the mouse. Its voice was, predictably, squeaky.

"You're not mighty," said Mole.

"True," said the mouse. "I'm not especially mighty. I *am* small, though. And that's handy for getting into small spaces."

"Oh, good," said Lily, near hysterical now, in an oddly calm sort of way. "Is that everyone, then?"

"No," said something slithering and smooth, winding itself around her feet. "There's me, too."

Lily looked down at the emerald-green grass snake, thin and sinuous, gazing up at her with hard little eyes.

Then, finally, Lily did what seemed like the only reasonable thing to do under the circumstances: she screamed.

And the curtains twitched in the upstairs window and slid open.

6

Lily threw herself to the ground and lay there, panting. Above her, the sky was purple. She watched the house. After a minute, maybe, the curtains closed again, and everything was dark. Smoke rose from the flue in the new kitchen roof, marrying the clouds above.

Lily flinched as the snake slid up her side and then coiled around her arm, until it was right by her face, looking into her eyes.

"You need to sssstay quiet," it said.

"I got that, thanks," said Lily in a whisper, not daring to move.

Mole and Mouse crept over. Lily noticed that they kept their distance from the snake.

She assembled the particles of her courage and looked

into the snake's reptilian eyes. "Are you . . . going to bite me?" she asked it.

The snake's tongue flickered in its mouth. "Not yet," it said.

"Not *yet*?"

"I mean no."

"There's a big difference between 'not yet' and 'no,' " said Lily.

"Oh, yes," said Mole, from somewhere near Lily's feet. "There are several more letters in 'not yet.'"

"It's natural to fear snakes," said Crow. "But don't worry. He is here to help you."

Lily sat up slowly. The snake didn't seem to be in any hurry to bite her and stayed still. The house was cold and black-windowed and showing no signs of life. Lily's blood, though, was still pulsing behind her eyes, her left eyelid twitching, and she was breathing hard.

She turned to face the house. "Have . . . have those things killed my parents?" she asked in a small voice. She could feel her last vestiges of hope—that this might be a dream—disappearing like wisps of mist do as the sun rises.

Only the sun was not rising, and it was still dark. So dark that the garden was a little world, encircled by nothingness.

"Oh, no, dear," said Mole.

"They can only get into empty houses," said Mouse. "Unprotected ones. If your parents had been home, they could not have come in."

"Unprotected ones?"

Mole bumbled over to the horseshoe and nudged it toward Lily with her nose.

Lily picked it up. It was heavier than it had any right to be, given its size. It was rough to the touch and looked like an old map, it was so rusted; archipelagoes of orange and white bloomed on the dark metal.

"Put it somewhere safe," said Mole. "Ready to hang it up again over the back doors, when this is over. They don't like iron."

Lily stood, being careful to move slowly, and went to lean the horseshoe against the paint tins. Gray Ground, the color in the nearest tin was called. Lily hadn't ever seen ground that was gray, and anyway, it looked like white paint—Lily knew that because it was the color on the new kitchen walls. She didn't understand why white paint was called gray. Her mind was babbling again, unable to still itself. Like a stream, flowing over rocks.

"So . . . what am I supposed to do?" she asked the animals.

"Get inside," said Mouse. "Defeat the replacements." He brandished the little needle sword. "Your parents won't be able to do it, and the baby will be in danger when it comes home."

"I don't care about The Baby. I don't want it." The words came out without any instruction from Lily's mind. She put her hand over her mouth, too late.

They all just looked at her, Mouse and Mole and Crow and, well, she supposed its name was probably Snake.

"I said I don't care about The Ba—"

"Yessss," said the snake. "We heard you."

"Get inside. Fight those things. Defeat them," said Mouse again, punctuating each sentence with a whisk of his needle sword.

Lily took a slow breath. "How do I do that?"

"How do you get inside? We'll help. We fly and tunnel and crawl into small spaces. Those are three of the ways into a house."

"That's not what I meant. I mean: How do I defeat them?"

"The answer," said Mole, "is inside you, my dear."

"Oh," said Lily. She looked down at herself. "Well, a fat lot of good that is." This was something her Granny Squeak sometimes said.

"No need to be rude," said Crow, preening. "We are here to help, not hinder."

Lily rubbed her eyes, thinking. "I don't know about fighting," she said. "But I do want to get inside. There's a note in there. On the kitchen table. It says where my parents are, where they're having The Baby. Maybe. There will be a phone number, anyway. If I can get the letter . . . I can go to them. My parents will know what to do."

"Really?" said Mole doubtfully. "Because they were the ones who took down the horseshoe."

Lily ignored her. "Plus," she said, "I want Willo." Suddenly and intensely, she longed to be in her own room, with her own things, with all its boring, comforting, wonderful familiarity.

"Who's Willo?" said Crow.

37

"A whale."

"You have a whale in your house?" asked Mole.

"Not a *real* one." Lily shivered as the words came out of her mouth. She had parents in her house that weren't real either.

The animals kept talking about whales and whether they had names, like dolphins, but Lily ignored them. She stood there in the dark and surveyed the exterior of the new kitchen, with its gleaming expanse of glass at the end, its bifold doors that were locked from the inside. But next to the kitchen was the top end of the *L*, the old kitchen, which was now a utility room. And at the end of *that* was a door, with a large dog flap in it.

"Has anyone seen a dog?" she asked.

Mole seemed to shiver. "I should hope not."

"He's only a spaniel," said Lily. "Buster. He sleeps in the utility room these days. I'm a bit allergic, and I'm . . . well, it's not good for me, him being too close. Also, Dad says dogs are good with babies, but Mum says they're good at slobbering and having fleas and smelling, too, and—"

She stopped, aware she was running on again, water-like, bubbling.

Then she felt something on her arm. She looked, and Mouse was scrambling up it, to her shoulder. His feet were little and clawed, and it made her skin prickle with goose bumps. He stood there next to her ear, watching the house. "You're thinking we try the doggie door?"

"Yes," she said, a little surprised. She supposed that *was* what she'd been thinking.

"Great!" He pricked the skin of her ear with the sword, and she yelped, but quietly, because she didn't want whatever was in the house to hear.

"First blood!" said Mouse. "Let's go!"

"First *blood*?" she said, touching her ear, which was sore.

"Yes. For luck, in battle. The sword must taste blood." He paused. "I think."

"You *think*?"

"Sorry," whispered Mouse.

Lily stood there, under the gray clouds, the squat black house in front of her, the utility room door ahead and to her right, with its large flap—just big enough for a small girl. Thinking about breaking in and actually doing it were two

different things, she was finding, and her body didn't seem to want to turn the first thing into the second.

"Or . . . we could stay here," she said.

"No," said Crow, landing on her other shoulder, with a soft touch of wing. "We must enter. And then the house will be clear, and your parents will return, with the baby, and you will be under your own roof, with people you love, who love you."

Lily thought that sounded nice. Apart from The Baby, but . . . well, if they came home, all of them, maybe she'd feel a bit less guilty about having wished away her parents. She thought back to her angry words to her mother, in the morning and in another life. She couldn't tell the animals all this was her fault.

"Okay," she said. She took a step forward.

Just then a single magpie flew past, black and white, and disappeared into the neighbor's garden.

"Oh no," said Lily. "That's not good, is it? As signs go?"

"What?" said Mole, looking around blindly. "What happened?"

"One magpie," said Lily. "Mum says: one for sorrow, two for joy."

"Silly," said Crow, still on her shoulder. "Not all birds

that fly in daylight and in moonlight have to mean anything. Some of them are just birds."

"Oh, good," said Lily.

Another magpie flew past, following the other.

"Thank goodness for that," said Crow.

"What? I thought you said it didn't mean anything?"

"We're going into unfathomable danger," said Crow. "Can't be too careful. Now, let's try to get through that flap in that door, shall we?"

7

Close up to the house, Lily could see the half-hearted Christmas decorations that were still up, even though Twelfth Night had long since passed, which was supposedly unlucky. She had a feeling the animals wouldn't like that, either, if they didn't like taking down horseshoes and seeing single magpies.

It had been a rubbish Christmas.

The pregnancy had done something to Lily's mum's back and knees—she mentioned her cartilage going softer, in preparation, which sounded monstrous to Lily. As a result, anyway, her mum had been too uncomfortable and awkward to do much, too aching and cumbersome, like a sea lion trying to navigate a house. She hadn't been able to cook because of all the bending down involved, so Lily's dad had done it and burned the Christmas dinner. Mum hadn't lifted up Lily to put the star on top of the Christmas tree, like she did every year.

Even the coal-eyed snowman had melted after only one night—the snow had not lasted for long.

Lily could see, in the new kitchen, the paper chain she herself had hung from hooks at the top of the floor-to-ceiling glass doors, the little fake miniature tree in the middle of the table, and some snowflake stickers she and her dad had put on the big glass windows—they peeled off, and you could use them again the next year. In fact, they were already peeling themselves off, from sunlight. Defeated and long overdue to be taken down.

She approached the other back door, the one to the utility room, with Crow on one shoulder and Mouse on the other, and Mole and Snake following.

There were two glass panels set into the top half of the door; Lily could see through them, to the utility room, which was dark and empty. The screens on the washing machine and tumble dryer were dim; nothing was on. Crow flew to the windowsill next to the door.

"Demon trap on this entrance, at least," he said.

"Huh?" said Lily.

Crow indicated something with his head. A spoked circle carved into the stones around the door. "Keeps those things out," he said. "So it's just the new kitchen that's the weak point. Old things are better. Much of this house is medieval, you see. More secure."

"It's all a bit academic, isn't it?" said Lily. She'd learned the word at school and was proud of using it.

"What does that mean?" said Mole. "Crow?"

"I . . . um . . ."

"Crow's clever," said Mole proudly. "He'll know."

"Maybe Lily should explain," said Crow.

"It means," said Lily, "that it doesn't really matter how they got in, they're in."

Crow puffed his feathers. "Might matter, at some point."

Lily crouched down, to the large flap at the bottom of the door. She was small, especially now; she'd fit through. She pushed the flap experimentally. It didn't move. Then she remembered: Buster, the dog, had a magnetic collar—the flap wouldn't open without it. To keep out foxes and things, or cats, from the neighbors. Not that there were any neighbors very nearby, Lily considered with a shudder. Though Lily's dad had said he wouldn't put it past the clientele of the Sherborne Arms to try to crawl through the flap.

Lily straightened up with a sigh. She was tired. She didn't have a watch, but she was sure she'd never been up this late.

"What's wrong?" asked Crow.

Lily explained about the collar.

"And it works with a magnet?" said Crow, from his position on the windowsill.

"Yes."

"Because aren't there lots of magnets on your fridge in there?" He was looking through the window, beak angled sideways.

Lily went to him. Yes. She should have seen herself: after all, the big steel thing provided the only light in the whole room, a pale green glow from the little screen on the refrigerator, which currently read:

Freezer: 18

Fridge: 3

And surrounding the screen, magnets: sparkly ones she'd got in her stocking, another shaped like a pizza from their favorite family restaurant, a stick figure you could dress up in different clothes, words on white tiles, all holding up letters from school, drawings, shopping lists. Words you were meant to make poetry with, words like:

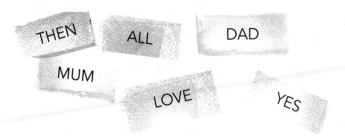

The fridge had been in the old kitchen, which was now the utility room, and it had stayed here; in the new kitchen extension there were built-in appliances, behind doors.

"Maybe one of those would open the flap," said Crow. "If someone could get inside."

"This is a job for me!" said Mouse. "Hold my sword." He shoved the needle toward Mole, not point-first luckily, who promptly dropped it.

"What was that?" said Mole, blindly.

"Sword," said Crow.

"Ah. Afraid these are digging hands," said Mole apologetically, raising them for inspection. "Not holding hands."

Mouse wasn't paying attention, though. He climbed up to the lower corner of the dog flap and, scrabbling with his back paws, pushed with his head and front paws until it opened a crack, bending against the lock in the middle, and then, quite suddenly, he popped through.

"Sword," he said from the other side. "Please."

"Why?" said Lily.

"In case of close-quarters combat."

"I don't think a needle is going to stop those things," said Lily. She recalled the hard black eyes, matte and unreflective. The unnatural movements. She wanted the note from her parents, but she wanted to get it without having to see the mother-thing again.

"I was thinking more of the dog," said Mouse.

"Oh." She wasn't sure she liked the idea of Buster being poked with a needle either, but she guessed it was preferable to Mouse being eaten. Buster couldn't talk, after all. As far as she knew.

Lily picked up the little needle and pushed it through the dog flap. It landed on the tiled floor on the other side with a little *ting* sound.

She went back to the window and watched Mouse scurry across the utility room floor, to the fridge, sword held in one paw. He reached up, stretched out as long as he could on his back paws, and pulled down a magnet shaped like a pineapple.

Then he ran back to the dog flap, fleet across the floor, and disappeared from view. A moment later there was a metallic click.

"Now," said Mouse.

Lily pushed her head through the flap and wriggled her shoulders through. The lip of it was hard against her stomach—she had to suck it in and hold her breath, eyes tightening with pain—but then she was through, landing in a sort of ungainly forward roll on the mat inside.

"Graceful," said Mouse.

"Watch it," whispered Lily, mindful of the parent-things, somewhere on the other side of the door. "Or I'll feed you to my pet owl."

"You have a pet owl?" squeaked Mouse, looking around.

"No. But I got you, didn't I? Okay, so there should be a note on the kitchen table," said Lily. "From my mum. It'll tell me where they are. We have to go through that door"— she indicated the door out of the utility room—"and then left, into the new kitchen."

"It doesn't matter where your parents are," said Mouse. "You need to defeat the replacements."

"I *need* to find that note."

He shrugged. Lily had never seen a mouse shrug. Mind you, she hadn't seen a mouse speak, either. Or carry a needle. "You're the boss," he said, shouldering the needle sword. "I mean, you're not, in this particular situation. You're very

49

much the underdog who is going to be lucky to get through tonight, even with our help. But it's a figure of speech."

"Wait," said Lily, stopping and looking down at him. "The underdog who . . ."

"Dog," said Mouse.

"Yes, you said that I was the underdog who—"

"No, *dog*. There."

Lily looked up again, and there was Buster, who had risen from some shadow in the corner of the room. He paced toward them, sniffing.

"Oh, hey, Buster," she said, putting out her hand to pet him on the head, like she'd always done, in the days before she got sick.

But the dog was bristling, his fur rising on end, and he was looking at her like she was a ghost, like she was someone he didn't know at all, and then he was charging toward her, snarling very loudly and throwing himself at her, claws out in front of him, jaws wide open to bite.

His eyes were very black.

8

L ily found herself, without particularly having decided to fall backward, on her bottom, hands out in front of her face. Buster wasn't a big dog, but as his teeth snapped down at her in slow motion, they seemed big enough.

She was going to lose fingers, her nose, an eye. It was amazing how quickly her mind was working, how flatly she thought these things. How accustomed to horror she was becoming. This was *Buster*, who loved her.

Then there was a flash of movement in front of her face, a glint of light on metal, and Mouse was suddenly standing on her nose, on Lily's nose, and Buster was tumbling away from them, backward, howling, tiny spatters of red blood popping into existence on the white tiles, his paws whacking clumsily at his muzzle.

"Lost my sword!" said Mouse. "Think it's stuck in there! But worth it!"

Lily stumbled to her feet, slippery-sliding toward the doggie door. Mouse jumped to the floor. The dog was still yowling, yipping, barking. "Got to get out," she said. "So loud."

The things were going to come. The parent-things were going to come. Her heart was a tightly wound metronome, the pendulum set to top speed, tick-ticking so quickly, so quickly. Piano: Lily had played it in a band with Scarlett, and Sofia had been a backup singer, which she was unhappy about. But not as unhappy as the audience would have been if she'd been lead singer, Lily had always thought.

That all seemed a long time ago, before her friends had started avoiding her, literally, like the plague.

She felt her way forward more than she looked with her eyes, terrified of what she might see, until she was at the dog flap. She pushed against it—mercifully, it swung out into the night, the lock only working one way; it didn't matter what left the house, it was only for stopping things getting in—and she felt the cold air on her face.

Then she remembered. "The note!"

"What?" said Mouse, behind her.

"My mum's note," she whispered. "I wanted to find it."

"It's on the table in the new kitchen, right?" said Mouse.

Lily nodded. "That's what Granny said."

"All right," said Mouse. "Yes! I'll go and get it, or I'll die trying."

He gave her a little salute with his paw and was off, streaking toward the door.

"Wait," she called after him. "Are those really the only two options?" But her voice went quiet toward the end, and her sentence guttered out like a candle in a draft as a sound came from the hall.

"Something's wound up the dog," went the sound.

It was her father's voice. Lily felt as if her heart might split in two, half of it wanting to hug him, the other half wanting to run far, far away.

"Maybe it's the girl, trying to get in," said the mother, from beyond the door. "If it is, get her."

"Oh, I will." Her father's voice again. Except it wasn't her father's voice, not quite. This one was as cold and flat as a sheet of steel.

With a grunt, Lily dived through the flap, scraping her tummy, landing on the wet gravel outside. She hauled herself sideways and into the deep darkness by the rainwater barrel.

Mouse was still in there. Mouse was still inside. Lily was surprised to find how much she didn't like that idea, even though she'd only just met him; how much she didn't want Mouse to get hurt.

She expected the utility room light to come on, for the window above her head to become a rectangle of orange brightness in the dark, but it didn't. She heard the dad-thing come into the room, the door opening, his steps sounding on the tiled floor, but he didn't seem to need light to see.

"Run, Mouse, run," said the crow, who was still standing on the windowsill, watching what was happening inside. Lily kept herself pressed against the wall.

"Oh, no," said Crow, dancing from little foot to little foot.

A scraping sound.

"No, no, not the broom," said Crow.

Was that a high squeak of fear from inside?

"Now run the *other* way," said Crow to Mouse, as if Mouse could hear. It was like when Lily's dad spoke to the players on the TV during a soccer game.

Lily couldn't stand it. She eased upward, unbending stiff knees, and lifted her head until she was peering through the bottom of the window. She could see her father, or the thing that looked like her father, moving almost like a dancer around the utility room, the long broom in two hands, twirling it, viciously sweeping the floor, and—there—the little scurrying form of Mouse, trying to avoid the bristles.

But her dad was fast, faster than her real dad, who occasionally cycled to the bakery for croissants on a Sunday and called it exercise, and the broom was twitching and switching and chasing Mouse across the floor like an enchanted object from a fairy tale. Her father's eyes were black and glittered dully, as if faceted. They weren't precisely round, either. Then Lily realized: they were made of coal. They were snowman eyes.

Fear expanded her chest painfully, like poisoned breath. Next to her ear, Crow flapped his wings in alarm.

"Honey," said her dad, over his shoulder. Her real dad had never called her mum "honey" in his life. Lily tucked away that information, in a little crease of herself. They were pretending to be her parents, but there were things they didn't know. That could be useful. "It's a mouse; I've got him cornered. Come and open the back door."

Lily ducked even lower as her black-eyed mum came smoothly into the room, the baby nestled under one arm. She glided to the back door and swung it open—Lily's dad whirled the broom, a blur, one side then the other, one side then the

other, so Mouse had nowhere to go but away from it, and then he said, "Ha!" as the broom head caught the little creature.

The door was open—with a flick, Lily's dad pushed the broom along and then up into the air, and from her vantage point against the back wall Lily saw Mouse go flying, a perfect arc of scrabbling legs pawing the air and squeaking and tail curling, and then crash into the new low wall dividing the patio from the garden.

The squeaking stopped. Lily was covering her mouth with her hands so she wouldn't make a sound; she didn't know when she had last drawn in breath.

"Did you see the girl?" said Lily's mum, still holding the door open.

"No sign of her."

"Good. She's a troublemaker. I could feel it. She seemed . . . determined. She might disrupt us."

"She's just a child," said Lily's dad. "She'll be alone. Scared. She's outside. We're inside. That's not going to change."

"And if it does?"

"Well," he said. "Children get broken very easily, don't they?"

With a light laugh, Lily's mum closed the door, and

there was a click as she locked it. Then Lily could hear footsteps receding as the two of them left the utility room. They locked the interior door to the utility room, too. The snick of it, metal against metal, was lighter, quieter, but still clear.

Lily ran over to Mouse and kneeled beside him. Crow landed with a flurry of wings next to her. Mole bumbled up behind and sat softly by her leg. Snake was somewhere nearby too; Lily could hear hissing.

Lily looked down at Mouse. He was lying very still, and very twisted, against the stone. She felt tears welling hotly in the corners of her eyes.

"Oh, Mouse," she said. "Oh, I'm so sorry."

Mouse didn't move.

9

Lily pressed her fists to her eyes. She couldn't believe this, any of it. She'd wished away her parents, told them that she never wanted to see them again, and now they were gone and things with coal eyes were in her home and Mouse was dead and it was all her fault. The other animals were crowded around her, heads bowed. Soft and furred; feathered. Apart from the snake.

"Sorry about what?" said Mouse, sitting up.

Lily fell back on her bottom; the gravel was damp, but she didn't mind. "Mouse! I thought you were dead. Why were you lying all still like that?"

"I was resting."

"*Resting?*"

"Yes. Took it out of me, all that running away from the broom."

Lily wiped her eyes with her sleeve. Another thing she couldn't believe: she couldn't believe she was crying over a talking mouse she hadn't even known before tonight. She felt a little silly for her overreaction. Mouse jumped up on her knee, ran up her body, and sat on her shoulder.

"What next?" he said.

"What do you mean, what next?"

"What next for getting in?"

Lily looked at the blank black house, all its doors and windows shut.

"You want us to go in there *again*?" she said.

"Don't you want your life back?" said Mouse.

Lily thought about this. She didn't want The Baby. But she did want to go back to how things were before, when it was just her and her mum and her dad, and holidays and drawing pictures and reading stories and playing at the playground, and all of them watching *Britain's Got Talent* together, before, when all she had to worry about was remembering her gym clothes on Mondays. Before she was sick.

But that was a lot to say.

"Yes," she said instead. Also, there was a little flicker of anger inside her, about what had happened to Mouse. Like the small flames when her parents lit the kindling in the cottage they sometimes rented in the Lake District. A glow. She hated other people being hurt; she'd always defended them. It was a thing her friends had said they liked about her, back when she still had friends.

Not that a mouse was a person. But still.

"We could always tunnel in," said Mole, from beside her.

"Aren't there . . . foundations and things?" said Lily. "Made of concrete?"

"Yes, that could be a problem," admitted Mole. "Oh, dear. I so wanted to help."

Just then there was a rustle from the bushes at the end of the garden. Lily turned to see a fox emerge, sniffing the air. "Let me guess," said Lily, turning to it. "He's going to get us in using cunning and guile."

"What?" said Crow.

"The fox."

"No," said Crow. "That's just a fox. And, anyway, it's a she."

"How can you tell?"

"Cubs."

And sure enough, as the fox crossed the garden, disappearing behind the wall on the other side, Lily saw three little cubs following. They looked just like the fox, only smaller. She supposed that to them, to the animals, she must look like her parents, like a small version of them, and that seemed to Lily as if it meant something, but she wasn't sure what.

"Anyway. I suggest we mount an assault from the air," said Crow, hopping up onto the wall, raising one wing dramatically.

"Meaning?"

"Meaning . . . we get in from above. Hang on."

Crow took off, and he flew high into the air above the house, his black wings bright with movement. For a few seconds he disappeared from view. Then he reappeared, landing on Lily's other shoulder.

"Chimney," he said.

"Right," said Lily. "What about it?"

"It's an old house," said Crow. "Big chimney. We can get up there, climb down it."

"I won't fit down a chimney," said Lily.

"You just went through a dog flap."

"Dogs are quite wide. Chimneys are not."

"Nonsense," said Crow, beak raised. "Children were

always going up and down chimneys in Victorian times, sweeping them."

"Were they, though?" said Lily. "Or is that just one of those things people say, that only actually happened, like, once maybe? Anyway, I really don't think I can squeeze down a chimney."

Crow pecked lightly at the skin of her neck.

"Well," he said. "Only one way to find out, isn't there?"

10

O f course, getting to the chimney meant getting up on the roof, and that was, as Lily's old dad, Lily's real dad, would have said, easier said than done.

The wall was very tall and wall-like. The windows were window-like: smooth expanses of glass. None of it was like stairs or like a ladder.

"Even if I could fit down the chimney, I can't get up there," said Lily.

"Nonsense," said Crow. " 'Can't' should not be in your vocabulary."

"That could cause a lot of problems," said Mole. "There would be a lot of things she couldn't express, to do with not being able to hear people or understand or—"

"It's a figure of speech," said Crow.

Snake hissed. "Here," he said, beginning to wrap himself around the bottom of a drainpipe. "Climb up this."

For a second Lily blinked at him. She had almost forgotten he was there. Why *was* he there?

"Yes!" said Mouse. "That will do it! Up the drainpipe!"

Lily looked at it. "I can't—"

"Tsk-tsk," said Crow.

Lily sat down on the little stone wall and rubbed away tears, angrily, with her arm. "But I *can't*," she said. "You don't understand. I'm no good at climbing now."

Mole roll-walked over to her and sat on her foot, in what might have been a cuddle. She was very soft and plump.

"Oh no," said Crow. "Mole is going to give one of her little pep talks."

"My dear," said Mole to Lily, ignoring Crow, "I can't see. I can't eat anything but worms. And do I complain about it?"

"Yes," said Mouse. "All the time."

"Hmm," said Mole. "I've lost the thread of my thought a little. Wait. I know." She tapped Lily's ankle with her long-clawed paw. "I can't see. I'm slow. Worms are disgusting. Those are things I can't change. But you *can* climb and you *can* defeat the replacements and you *can* have your life back."

"Actually, that was surprisingly good," said Crow. "Though I disagree about worms—if you find a particularly juicy one, they're . . ."

Lily wasn't listening. She was thinking about what Mole had just said. No one ever told her she could do things anymore. Especially not her parents and Granny Squeak. They were always telling her not to do stuff. To rest. To preserve her strength. She knew they meant well, but it was almost as exhausting as the illness.

She patted Mole's furry little head and stood, going over to the drainpipe, which shone plastic-black against the whitewashed wall. Crow flew up and landed on the flat roof of the kitchen extension above her.

"Once you're up here," he said, "you can reach the gutter and lift yourself up onto the sloped roof with the tiles. Then it's just an easy climb up to the chimney."

"Oh, is that all?" muttered Lily. But the thought of the note, from her mum, was a spur in her side, shiny and sharp.

She reached up and got her fingers around one of the horseshoe-shaped brace parts that bolted the drainpipe to the wall, then pulled up while lifting her foot to rest on a lower one. She stretched up, keeping her weight close to the wall, fingers throbbing with the effort of it.

Another handhold. Another foothold. She was halfway up to the roof now.

Her fingers slipped, and she slid down a short way, scraping her knee and shin on the ridged pipe, skinning one of her knuckles. But she managed to hold on so she didn't slide all the way back down to the ground. Her head felt unmoored from her body, bobbing and turning, as if she were on a ship, not pressed against something flat and solid.

Lily cursed. She'd been good at climbing. She'd been the one to show Sofia and Ella, whose family had moved away to Birmingham, how to get *up* the fireman's pole at the playground, swinging her legs up so that she was almost upside down, her feet on the platform at the top, then walking her hands up the pole.

Not anymore. Now she was weak.

Now she was rubbish at everything.

She was even rubbish at being ill. She had a whole team of doctors, including a therapist, and the therapist—"just Dan, no titles here"—was always talking about "illness narratives" (he made bunny ears in the air with his fingers for the quote marks), and how people who accepted that they were chronically sick did better than those who didn't, and how Lily wasn't "authentically living" her life because she was still grasping on to how things used to be.

Lily didn't think that was terribly surprising, seeing how much better things used to be, even two years ago. She'd had energy, for one thing, and friends, and a mum who wasn't always distracted and anxious, waddling like a great pregnant hippo, and she hadn't had to keep going to the hospital to be hooked up to a giant bleeping machine. Hospitals spoke in bleeps, Lily had learned. Some days it was all she heard for hours—different pitches, from different bits of apparatus, flashing their lights, beeping regularly or intermittently.

Once, there had been a long, continuous beep and lots of people in green scrubs came running, but that was only because Lily had gotten bored and taken the pulse and oxygen monitor off her thumb. Dan had talked a lot about acceptance after that, and also after the time she ran away when Dr. Kothari wanted to inject her with something, and they'd found her in the Caffè Nero in the main lobby, hiding behind the cooler unit with all the paninis in it.

But. But there were *things* in her house that didn't belong there, and she wasn't going to accept that, either. Or being kept away from her mum's note and her mum and dad.

Ignoring the pain in her shin and knee, she began to

climb again. Eventually, she was able to get her hands on the flat roof of the new kitchen, then haul herself, one leg at a time, up and onto the rough, black, waterproof surface of it.

"Took your time," said Crow, head cocked to one side.

"I don't have wings," she said.

"I know. Too bad for you. They're very handy."

She ignored him and edged round the wall side, nervous of falling. She went past the big skylight, which she forced herself not to look down through, in case something was looking back up at her, then up to the stone wall of the original house. Just above her was the gutter and overhang of the main, sloping roof. It was tiled with old slates, lumps of green moss growing between them. Sometimes when her family was watching TV at night, a piece of moss would come loose, from a bird walking around or something, and roll down and hit the ground, and they'd all be startled, her mum especially.

Lily would love to go back to when the only scary thing about the house was moss.

She hooked her fingers on the gutter and levered herself up, so that one leg was lying in it, lengthwise, then sort of rolled herself up so that all of her was half on the roof and half in the gutter, which was damp and full of wet leaves.

Her jeans and hoodie were damp now too. It was not comfortable.

Carefully, she inched up the roof, keeping herself flat against it, so that she was lying on her tummy against the tiles. She was cold and anxious and it was dark, but she took all that and used it as fuel. To get herself inside, where it was warm. To get back to her real parents, so they could help her fix whatever was wrong with the house.

Slowly, slowly, she crawled up the angled roof, using the thick moss as handholds. The chimney seemed far above, unreachable almost, a black silhouette against the clouded sky.

"Quarter of the way there now!" said Crow. "Well done."

"That isn't helping," said Lily through teeth that were clamped together so tight, her jaw ached.

Her breath was coming hard and ragged, and the water from the gutter had soaked through to her clothes now. She'd felt like this once before, walking home to their holiday cottage in the Lake District, after her dad got them lost out in a field somewhere. But then there'd been hot chocolate and a fire waiting for her, whereas now . . . now she had to face fake parents who were really, what? Ghosts?

Vampires? *Demons?* That was the word the animals had used, about the wheel carved into the stone of the house. Demon trap.

She shivered, the tingling sensation racing through her limbs, and the piece of moss she was clinging to tore away from the roof, like they sometimes did when she and her parents were watching TV. But this time she was holding on to it, and she slid down the roof with a yelp.

11

Lily caught the gutter, legs dangling in the air.

Oddly, what she thought of was a wooden toy her granny had in her house—a monkey that you could hang from shelves in different ways; from its feet or its hands or its tail. She was the monkey, and she was hanging by her hands.

Fear was a fist around her heart. She didn't want to fall. *Please don't let me fall. Please don't let me fall.* It went round in her head like a nursery rhyme.

"What's happening?" said Mole from below. "Oh, I wish I could see! Is she all right!"

"Oh, yes," said Mouse. "She's hanging on the gutter and flailing around a bit, but her foot is only about an inch above the kitchen roof. I think she's forgotten about the new bit of the building."

Lily glanced down. This was true. Oh, dear. Even in front of animals, she was embarrassing herself.

Sighing, she got ready to climb again. She wondered, in a small, calm part of her mind, why Mouse and Mole were happy to shout, why it wouldn't risk warning the parent-things that she was there, trying to get in. But maybe it just sounded like animal sounds to them.

Muscles burning, she heaved her weight forward and upward till her elbows were on the gutter too, bone-aching sore, and then she wriggled her torso up and onto the roof again.

The crow stood on a tile close by.

"Not a word," she said.

"I wasn't going to say anything," he said.

With Crow hopping beside her, she started to crawl up again, testing each clump of moss this time, trying to ensure it would hold her weight before she pulled herself up. It felt like hours passed, but it was probably only minutes, and then she was sitting astride the angle of the roof, one leg on each side. In front of her the wide chimney rose into the night air, nearly as tall as she was. She could see the low hills on the horizon, their outlines blurred with trees.

Just then two magpies flew past, low. The same ones from earlier, maybe, though Lily wouldn't have been able to tell. And as they disappeared into the blackness of the night, a feather fell, and Lily put out her hand, flat, and the feather floated down onto it. Black, fading to white at the end.

"Keep that," said Crow. "Powerful charm."

"Right. Okay," said Lily. She was past questioning that sort of thing. She put the feather into her jeans pocket.

Crow flapped up onto the top of the chimney with a clatter of wings, then stalked around the outside, muttering. Above, the stars twinkled, and the gray line of an airplane contrail scarred the sky.

"What is it?" Lily asked.

"There's a grille," he said.

"A grille?"

"Yes, a metal barrier, to stop birds from getting in, making nests and so on."

"Oh," she said. "Ironic."

"Why?"

"Well, you're a bird. And we're trying to get in."

Crow harrumphed. "I'm not the type of bird that makes nests in chimneys. I'm not *stupid*."

"I should think not," said Lily. "What with the fire and the smoke."

"Look, it was *one time*," said Crow. "Hundreds of years ago. And my feathers were only lightly singed. The point is, I learn my lessons."

Lily turned away, so he wouldn't see her smile. Then the smile petered out as she remembered about the grille. She shuffled along to the chimney and pulled herself up to a standing position, her stomach only whooshing lightly when she saw the drop to the road on the other side of the roof.

The grille on the chimney looked ancient, made of iron. She stared at it.

"Wait," she said.

"What?"

"*Hundreds* of years ago?" she asked.

"We're old," said Crow. "Old things are good. They knew how to make things in the old days. Including us. Focus on the grille."

She seized the bars and pulled at it. Nothing happened. It was strong.

"See?" said Crow. "In the old days they knew how to keep out bad things."

"I thought it was to keep out birds."

"Objects can have more than one purpose. A locked door keeps out people. Carve a spoked circle on it, like the one by the utility room, and it will keep out demons, too. *This* stops them from getting down the chimney."

"And us."

"Well, yes. Unfortunately."

She seized the grille and shook it angrily, and to her surprise, this time it broke immediately, the bar coming away in her hand. Her other hand shot out to prevent any of the metal from falling down the chimney and alerting the things living in her house.

"Rusty," she said. "I guess not all old things are good."

"Humph," said Crow. "In you go, then."

"Just . . . in the chimney? Like that?"

"Well, I don't know, I don't have arms, I'm not sure how it works."

"I've never climbed down a chimney."

"First time for everything."

Lily rolled her eyes. "That's a stupid expression. If I jumped off a cliff, it would be my first time. And my last."

"This isn't a cliff."

"No. It's a chimney. There might be a fire at the bottom."

The crow shook his head, which wasn't something Lily had thought crows could do. "No. Those creatures, they don't like heat or light."

"Oh." Lily put this away, another small piece of knowledge, in another crease of herself.

"Besides. No smoke."

Lily sighed. No more excuses. She pulled herself up to a perch on the lip of the chimney, then dangled her legs inside.

The only thing she could think to do was to brace herself against the sides with her feet and hands, so that was what she did. The stone brickwork scraped her skin, especially her soft palms, and the soot made her sneeze. It echoed loudly in the chimney. She stopped for a moment.

Silence.

She continued moving, slowly, down. There was a flutter above her, and then sharp little claws dug into her scalp, followed by the impression of a soft bottom on her hair.

"Are you sitting on my head?" she whispered.

"Yes. Whatever you wash your hair with doesn't smell very nice."

"Oh, *sorry*," she said, more brittle than she intended, what with the heart-tightening fear. "When this is all over, I'll change it."

"That would be for the best," Crow said, oblivious to sarcasm.

Lily lowered herself down bit by bit, darkness closing in as the top of the chimney receded above her. She felt that the stone walls were getting closer, pressing in, squeezing her, so that her breaths came shallow and fast, but she didn't know if that was just her imagination.

Then she noticed light from below her—only dim light, but light all the same. It brightened gradually, and then her right foot hit open air instead of chimney, and she paused, confused. She couldn't be anywhere near the fireplace in the living room yet.

She kept going down, and an opening grew in front of her, square. She could see carpet in the moonlight. Her parents' bedroom! This was the little fireplace in her parents' bedroom, which they had never lit. It must join to the same chimney.

But was it big enough to crawl out?

She lowered herself down below the opening, so that she could go headfirst.

"You go before me," she whispered.

With a whirl of wings, Crow disappeared through the hole.

Lily climbed up and squeezed herself wormlike through it, hunching her shoulders as narrow as they'd go, her vision filled by grate and carpet and the patterned edge of her parents' bed throw.

And then she was out! Tumbling gracelessly into the grate and onto the bedroom floor.

She stood.

She looked around.

And . . .

Her mother was standing there, in the starlight spilling through the window, holding a baby in one arm and Crow, by the throat, in the other. Her black coal eyes were drawing in what little light there was, sucking it up.

"Hello, errant daughter," she said.

12

Lily stood rock-still, ice-still, still as the water in a deep well far underground.

"This is becoming tiresome," said her mother who was not her mother. The woman's coal eyes were very black and had more sides than eyes should. She was wearing Lily's mother's clothes, her old flowery dress, and that put a hot anger into Lily's throat, burning.

The baby in the woman's other arm never moved. Come to think of it, Lily hadn't seen it move at all. Maybe it wasn't even a baby the mother-thing was holding. Well, it couldn't be. The Baby wasn't here yet. A thought appeared in Lily's mind, as surprising as a frog in a bath. She wasn't going to let these *things* stop her from meeting her little brother or sister.

"Get out of my house," said Lily, and then blinked, startled that the words had come out of her mouth.

"No," said the mother-thing. "We live here now. You are not needed."

"*I* live here," said Lily.

"Oh, do you? Then why are you climbing down the chimney like a thief in the night?" Flick, flick, went her eyes.

"I . . ."

"You are an interloper. You must leave."

"When my parents get back from the hospital . . ." Lily trailed off. She had been about to say, *with the new baby*, but that, it seemed, was something she couldn't say. "When my parents get back, they'll kick you out."

"Don't be silly," said the mother. "They won't see us. Maybe they will come in, but then as time goes by, they will get sick, and die, and never know why. The baby will see us. But it won't be able to say anything, not until it's too late. And *you* will be gone."

"I won't."

"You will, if you know what's good for you. Even if you stayed and you told your parents, what do you think would happen? Do you think they would believe you?"

Lily blinked, considering. She could imagine what might

happen if she told Call-Me-Dan that there were invisible demons in her house. She'd probably find herself seeing more doctors, other doctors. Doctors for her head.

"You see?" said the mother-thing. "*Leave.*" The word was like a sound from beyond the stars, from another world, and it snapped Lily back to where she stood in the little room.

"Won't." Lily stamped her foot. She hadn't done that since she was little. Then a thought chimed in her mind. "Wait," she said. "My parents weren't here. So you came in, and you look like them. But *I* wasn't here either. Why isn't there one of you that looks like me?"

The mother-thing cocked its head, with a gruesome smile that was very unlike her real mother's. "Why would we want to do that? Who wants a broken child who needs lots of injections and pills? Far better to start again with the new one."

Lily's eyes flickered to the baby, which remained silent and still. She took in a sharp breath. "Get. Out. Of. My. House," she said. But her voice was shaky.

The mother let out what might have been a sigh. "You know, if you're going to keep creeping about, trying to sneak in, we don't just have to kill you or kick you out. There is another choice. A choice *you* could make."

"Which is?"

"We absorb you."

"You absorb me?"

"Yes." The mother waved a hand at Lily's body. "We take your life force, suck it out of you. Your . . . suffering would end. You would become a part of us. In a way you would live forever."

"In a way?"

"Well. In another way you would be dead."

Lily blinked.

"You would only have to let us hug you," continued the mother.

"Hug you," echoed Lily's father, standing at the door in the half-light. None of the bulbs in the house were lit. "Hug you and hug you, tighter and tighter, until you can't breathe anymore."

"And then we would breathe our own breath into you, and you would be one of us, and you'd never have to see a doctor again," said the mother.

"Because I would be dead."

"Yes."

"No," croaked the crow, from his stranglehold in the mother's closed fist. "Say no."

But Lily was tempted. Oh, in a small way she was tempted. No more hospital visits, no more tests, no more injections, no more sucking out all her blood and washing it and dripping it back in, with machines bleeping all the while.

No baby.

The mother squeezed Crow's throat, and he gave out a thin, distressed squawk.

Lily took a breath. Her hurting was one thing, her having needles stuck in her was one thing, but she couldn't see Crow rasping for breath. *"No,"* she said. "And let go of my friend."

"Very well, then," said the mother. "Time to leave." She nodded to Lily's father-thing, who strode surprisingly quickly into the room and scooped Lily up by the waist and threw her over his shoulder.

"What are you doing with me?" Lily screamed.

"You're rubbish; you're junk; you're not wanted; you're a small, sick thing," he said.

And Lily said nothing, because those things were true; those things were all true and what she was.

He was silent for a moment. And in that moment, as he carried her, Lily realized something else through the fog of

her panic, something else these imposters had gotten wrong: he didn't lisp, unlike her real father, who had learned to speak when he couldn't hear properly, before there were cochlear implants.

Not that this information did her any good.

He kicked the bedroom door wide open and held her tight. "So I'm throwing you out," he finished.

13

The father-thing carried her through the doorway, stronger than her own father could ever be, and she banged her head on the lintel, but he didn't stop when she cried out. He crossed the hall, past the big glass bowl on the hall windowsill that held Lily's courage beads. These were colored beads on a string necklace—Lily earned one every time she went to hospital, which was a lot. She wasn't sure what she was supposed to do with them, though; she had no intention of wearing the necklace. Which was why it was in a bowl in the hallway.

Then her replacement dad turned jerkily and took her into what was going to be The Baby's bedroom; Lily had watched her dad paint it yellow because they didn't know if The Baby was a girl or a boy yet. She'd refused to help.

The mother was behind them, still holding Crow, following. Crow's eyes were shifting from side to side, hunting for an escape, any escape, but there was none.

From her vantage point on the demon father's shoulder, Lily could also see her shoes. Her real mother's shoes. Her mum would hate that—the fact that the creature was wearing them at all, but also that she was wearing them *in the house*. Lily's mum didn't think shoes belonged on feet in houses.

Lily's fake dad strode right through the room past the newly built chest of drawers with a built-in diaper changer and the crib, and then he swung the window open.

"Oh no, oh no, oh no," said Lily, who had an idea of what was about to happen. But he ignored her. He pushed her through the window, and she landed with a bang on the scaffolding, which rattled worryingly, and then he was on his feet next to her, and he picked her up again. The mother stepped through the window, legs high, insectlike, after them.

The father lifted Lily up, and she was high, high above the ground, high even above the scaffolding.

"Please don't," she said.

But he ignored her, and he pushed her headfirst into the rubbish chute. Then he let go.

She slid, as fast as on a slide, banging her elbows painfully on the sides when the pipe turned, and there was a swinging sensation in her stomach, lurching, and she shot out the other end and landed in the garbage dumpster, half on a broken mattress, which was a mercy, and half on a pile of broken-up floorboards, which wasn't.

"Ow," she said. She was covered in dust.

A black object flew out of the chute after her and smacked her in the face before falling to the mattress, where it lay limply, wings spread out, covered in soot and dotted with spatters of paint and other, less identifiable things.

"Well, that was a soft landing at least," said Crow.

"Not for me, it wasn't," said Lily, rubbing her face where his claws had smacked into her nose and cheek.

"No. But for me," he said. "Which is what counts, after all."

Lily climbed out of the trash bin with a sigh, dirty, disheveled, and something else beginning with *d*.

Defeated, maybe.

Crow flew out, but not for long—one of his wings didn't quite flap, and he rose above the rusted edge of the dumpster, spun in the air a bit, not elegantly, and then nose-dived into a rosebush.

"*Thorns,*" he said crossly.

"Serves you right," said Lily. But she went and picked him up anyway. Inside she was shaky and relieved to still be alive, even if she didn't want to show it to Crow. "Your wing. Is it broken?"

He sat in her hands and flexed it experimentally. "I don't think so," he said. "Just hurt. I wasn't expecting it. What now, then?"

"What do you mean, what now?" said Lily.

"What's the plan? For getting in and defeating the replacements."

Lily looked down at herself. At the dirt and the bruises. Then she looked at the cold, dark house. "Do I have to?" she said.

"No. Yes," said the crow.

"Not helpful."

The crow gave her a significant look down his beak. "And yet. It has to be you."

Lily sighed. "I still think my parents will know what to do. But I'd have to get that note, from the kitchen table." Actually, Lily had no idea if her parents would know what to do, but finding the note gave her a purpose, albeit a seemingly impossible one, whereas the idea of defeating the things, whatever that meant, was . . . scary.

Crow pecked her hand lightly. "Could you put me on your shoulder? I'd feel more dignified."

She realized she was cradling him, like a cuddly toy. She raised him up to her shoulder, and he perched there, digging his feet in more than she'd have liked, but she didn't say anything. He had just had quite an embarrassing fall.

"Thank you," he said. "So. The kitchen table. I think, rather, that it must be Mole's turn."

"Mole's turn?"

"To get you into the kitchen, of course."

"Oh," said Lily. She turned and looked up at the house, forbidding, squat, gazing blindly back at her with its black windows. She shuddered. "Yes, I suppose." A car drove past, lights sweeping against the hedges on the other side of the road as it turned. A strange visitor from a world where magic didn't exist—like a submarine all lit up on the black ocean floor.

Lily watched it go, till the red rear lights were only lingering ghosts on her retinas, floating.

Then she turned back to the house.

14

They took the side route to the back garden, Lily careful not to trip the security light on the shed. There, Mole and Mouse and Snake were waiting for them.

"You're all dirty," said Mouse.

"Really?" said Lily. "I hadn't noticed."

"Goodness," said Mouse. "But you're covered in black soot and paint and . . . and that white dusty stuff . . . and something that looks like cream, but it seems odd you'd have come across any cream, so—"

"Wallpaper glue, I think," said Lily flatly. "And I know. I was being sarcastic."

"Oh, it sounds *awful*," said Mole. "I wish I could see."

"It sounds awful, but you want to see?" said Mouse.

"Well, yes," said Mole. "It still sounds quite interesting. And, anyway, it's not me covered in all those things. It's Lily."

"Thanks," said Lily.

Crow jumped from her shoulder and flew a little stiffly to the ground.

"Oh, dear," said Mouse. "Are you injured?"

"Nothing serious," said Crow, almost as stiffly as he had moved. "I'll be fine." He puffed his chest self-importantly.

"Sssssoooo," said the snake. "What are we going to do now?"

"It's Mole's turn, according to Crow," said Lily, sitting down on the damp grass.

"Ah," said Mole.

"Do you . . . have any ideas?" said Lily.

"We'll have to dig," said Mole.

Lily looked at the cold ground. The idea could not be more unappealing. She lay back on the grass. There was a light breeze. The house was a cutout against the night; a darker shape on a dark background.

"Or we just stay here," she said.

"What?" said Mouse.

"I mean . . . we could just give up. Maybe it's not worth

95

it. I'll just . . . live out here, with you guys or something." She wasn't sure she could face the parent-things again. Or being thrown out of the house like garbage, which was the thing she'd feared for so long anyway, come true. The idea of it had scared her even more since her real mother's stomach had started to grow and then pulse with the movements of a new baby.

A replacement baby.

Still lying on her back, Lily looked up at the night sky. The moon had gone away, behind a cloud. From this angle, the house was huge in front of and above her, surrounded by the dark, wearing it. As if the darkness didn't belong to the sky but to the house; as if the house were creating it, pumping it out from its windows.

Crow walked over to her, flexing his injured wing. Lily had never seen a bird wince, but his whole way of being was the word "wince" transformed into movement. "But the note," he said. "You want to find your parents. You just said."

Lily shrugged. It was as if the dampness of the grass were getting into her skin, her bones, making her soft and loamy, unwilling to move, like the ground itself.

It wasn't, though. It was something else: it was guilt seeping into her bones, into her muscles. The knowledge that she'd done this, when she'd told her parents she never wanted to see them again. She'd brought the things into the house; that was why she couldn't move.

"You have to defeat the replacements!" said Mouse.

"You keep saying 'defeat,'" said Lily with a sigh. "Why not just say 'kill' and be done with it? I don't want to kill them. I can't kill them. They're too strong."

"Oh, they can't be killed, dear," said Mole.

"Brilliant," said Lily, throwing up her hands. "Even more reason to give up."

Snake curled around her foot. "Your sssssister will die," he said.

Lily stared at him. Sister? What? What sister? Oh, The Baby. The Baby was a . . . what? Wait. *Die?* It was going to die? Oh no. Her mind was babbling again, being water, no longer solid. Slipping away from her.

"Sister?" she said at last.

"The baby," said the snake. "Your parents will bring her home, and she will die."

"We don't know if it's a boy or a girl," said Lily. "My parents didn't find out." Her mum, crouching in front of her with the strip of photos: *We wanted it to be a surprise, a kind of present for all of us.*

"Oh," said Snake. "Well. We do."

"We know things," said Crow.

"Not useful things," said Lily.

Crow blinked. "*Some* useful things."

"Okay, tell me how to defeat those things, if you're so useful."

"The answer is—"

"Yes, yes, inside myself. Like I said, not useful."

Crow made a tutting sound.

"I don't care anyway," said Lily. Though it gave her a tingle, like pins and needles in her heart, the idea of a sister. "Let her die."

The animals were silent.

"I said, let her die."

Still silent.

"I said . . . I said . . ."

But Lily found that she couldn't say, couldn't say anything. There were tears in her eyes.

"I don't want any of this," she said in a very small voice; she wasn't even sure they would hear her. "I just want to go back to how things were before." At the same time she knew it was bad to never allow herself to live *now*, to always be thinking of a past before she was ill, or a future where she wasn't anymore and where, somehow, miraculously, there was no Baby at all. It was bad because it meant she was never *here*, really, she was always in some murky place where time didn't really exist. It was like living on the bottom of the sea, with the octopuses.

"Before what?" said Crow.

"Pardon?" said Lily, who had been elsewhere. On the seabed. Shells all around her.

"You said you wanted to go back to how things were before. So I said, before what?"

She nodded. "Before The Baby. Before I got sick."

"You don't look sick," said Mouse.

"But I am."

"Will you die?" said Mole, shuffling closer to her.

"Yes. If I can't get a transplant, I might."

"*Might,*" said Crow. "And for now you are alive. Right?"

"Yes," said Lily slowly.

"But the baby *will* die. If you don't get into that house and fix things."

"Or get my parents to help," said Lily.

The animals were silent again.

Lily stood, blowing out her cheeks. The moon had come out from behind the clouds. It was bright and blue and seemed like a sign of something that Lily couldn't have put into words. But then that was the whole point of signs.

The ground was cold and wet underfoot; her jeans were soaked. But, apparently, she wasn't someone who just gave up. Even if she slightly wished she were.

The animals looked up at her expectantly, gathered around her, in a half circle. Lily let the air out of her cheeks, cross with herself. The problem was, she wasn't someone who could lie, either.

"It's just . . . there's something I haven't told you," she said.

"Being?" said the crow.

"Being . . . that it's my fault. It's all my fault. I told my parents I never wanted to see them again—it was the last thing I said to them—and that's why this has happened, that's why those things are there, it's—"

"—not your fault," interrupted the snake.

"What?" Lily said, looking down. Her cheeks were wet with tears.

"Words don't matter," said the crow. "Well. They do—that's what spells are made of, after all. But words can't bring the demons. Only leaving a house unprotected can do that."

"Spells aren't real," said Lily.

"Really?" said Crow. "Try telling someone you forgive them. That you love them. Or that you *don't* forgive them. That you hate them. Spells are very real."

Lily blinked.

"None of this is your fault," said Mouse. "But you can put it right."

Lily blinked again. That sounded good. Wait. Was that a spell, on her? To get her to do what they wanted?

Maybe it was.

Maybe it didn't matter.

"Anyway," said Mole, "strictly speaking, there's something we haven't told you either."

15

E r . . . ," said Lily. "What?"

"*Mole,*" said Crow angrily.

"Ssspectacular," said the snake. "Ssspectacular idea, Mole. Sssshe was jusssst about to do it."

"*What haven't you told me?*" said Lily, her voice very cold, very precise, ringing like air on ice.

The crow flapped painfully up onto her hand, wing still not beating right. "It's not bad," he said. "The thing we haven't told you."

"So what is it?"

"It's us," said the mouse, from Lily's foot. He was leaning against it, looking sad.

"Ussss," said the snake.

"We . . . ," began the crow. He gestured with his wing,

at the garden. "Out here we have the power," he said. "In there . . ." He indicated the house. "In there they do."

"Okay . . ."

"But when your family did that"—he pointed to the extension—"you brought some of the *outside* into the *inside*. Specifically . . . the well."

Lily stared at the black box of the kitchen, its big bifold doors, the wooden floors beyond and the kitchen island. She remembered: they'd found an old well under the patio, and the housing association had gotten involved; there'd been talk of filling it in, but there was nowhere in the water table for the water to go, and there was also an idea that it might have been collecting rain in a way that was actually protecting the house from flooding—plus, it was very sturdily built, narrow at the top and wide at the bottom, full of clear water. The building inspector said it was very ancient, that it had probably been there, stone-walled and silent, collecting fresh water from the hills for hundreds of years.

Lily had felt dizzy looking into it.

So, in the end, it had been decided that it was more trouble than it was worth to try to get rid of it. The builders had capped it off and done the concrete screeding atop it, then laid the wooden floor over that. Apparently, it was totally secure.

"*You could put in a glass floor section,*" one of the builders had suggested. "*Show off the well to your visitors.*"

"*I'd rather hide it, thank you very much,*" Lily's mum had said. "*I'm pregnant, my daughter's very ill, and that well has held us up by four weeks and cost us tens of thousands. I'd blow it up if I could.*"

Now Lily imagined the well, under the floor. The big pool of still water, unseen. Black. When she'd looked into it, all the way down, she had felt trembly and cold, head turning in a way that made her stagger. She was glad it was covered up.

"So," she said to the animals now, "the well came inside. And that means . . . ?"

"Yes," said Crow. "It means."

"Means . . . what?"

"A lot."

Lily took a long, patient breath. These creatures. She weighed the little black bird on her hand. "What. Does. It. Mean?" she said.

"They have the source," said Mouse.

" 'Sauce' with an *au* or 'source' with an *ou*?" asked Lily, who didn't have the benefit of seeing the word written down.

"I don't know," said the mouse. "I'm a mouse," he added after a moment, not unreasonably.

"S-o-u-r-c-e," the crow spelled out. "The source of . . . us. Our magic. Good magic. All of it."

"It'ssss inside now," said Snake. "With them."

"The *source of all magic* is under my house?" said Lily. "Why . . . why would it be there?"

"Why not?" said Mole.

Lily didn't have an answer for that. "Why does it matter, though?" she said. "It's under, like, five inches of concrete."

"It matters because *they* are in your house," said Crow. "Their presence will . . . poison the water. We will die."

"Let me get this straight," said Lily. "The Baby will die. My parents will die. You will die. And I'll be . . . what? Out here on my own? In the dark. Like a . . . like a banished ghost or something?"

"Yes," said the crow sadly.

"Yesss," said the snake, probably sadly, though it was a bit hard to tell with the hissing.

"Yes," said the mouse. "So let's not let that happen!" He struck a heroic pose.

"Bring on death, say I," said the mole. "No more eating worms."

Lily stifled a giggle, despite herself. This was all so absurd, and they were all so silly, and . . . she wasn't going to let them die. The knowledge surprised her. No matter how terrifying the fight might be, she was going to do it.

So.

She cricked her neck, looking at the walls of the house. "Okay, then, Mole," she said. "What have you got? How are we getting in there?"

Mole bumbled over to her, long nails scraping against grass. "I have . . . an inkling of an idea," she said.

"Right," said Lily to Mole. "What is it?"

"Well, while you and Crow were gone, I dug around a little. Followed my nose. It led me to some worms, actually, that were slightly less revolting than usual, not too moist, not too dry, nicely plump, so I ate some of them, and then I found some more, and—"

"And you found something more helpful than worms?" prompted Lily, who found Mole cute but wanted her to get to the point so they could get inside and end this.

"Nothing more helpful than a worm if you're peckish," said Mole. "And digging is tiring work. But, yes, actually."

"Which is . . . ?"

"There's an old coal chute, or something like it," said

Mole. "Under the end of the old part of the house, near the dog flap. It goes into the cellar—in the olden days people used to pour coal down there by the barrow-load. More efficient than carrying it."

"Quite ingenious, really," said Crow. "Folk knew what they were about, back then. Coal chutes, horseshoes above doors, circles carved in the stone to—"

"Yes, yes," said Lily. "But it's a way in, right?"

"I think so," said Mole. "It's been covered up—someone put a slab of stone over it and then piled it with earth. But it's still there."

"Where?"

"Here," said Mole, waddling over to the ground just in front of the utility room—or the old kitchen, as Lily kept thinking of it. "I can dig away the earth. You'll have to move the stone."

Lily glanced down at her bony arms. "I'm not sure I can do that."

"You're the only one here who can even try," said Mole.

Lily thought of what her mother and grandmother

would say. How they'd tell her to rest, to save her strength: *Leave it for us to do, Lily. You must be exhausted, Lily. You look pale.*

She set her jaw. "All right, then," she said.

So Mole began to dig. Earth flew into the sky and became black rain. She worked quickly, turning, kicking mud up into a little hill with her spadelike back paws, cutting through it with her sharp front claws. Soon a wide, square piece of stone became visible, scratched by her digging.

Lily bent down, got her fingers under the edge of it, and tried to shift it to the side. It didn't move.

"Try lifting," said Mouse. "Topple it over."

"Easy for you to say."

"It isn't, actually. 'Topple' is quite tricky for a mouse. The *p* sound, when you don't have lips, is—"

He saw the way she was looking at him and shut up.

Lily bent her knees this time, so she was crouching, and got both hands under the slab. She ignored the voices of her parents, her granny, telling her she couldn't do it. She surged upward, holding the stone, and sure enough, the side popped out of the ground with a sucking sound, then it teetered on its edge for a second before falling down hard on the gravel, revealing a mouthlike opening beneath, lined with dark bricks.

Mouse dodged out of the way just in time. "A bit of warning wouldn't go amiss!" he said.

"You literally just told me to do that," said Lily.

"Well, yes, but I didn't think you'd actually be strong enough."

"Sssstop," said the snake. "Sssshadows. In the house."

They all looked up. Something flickered past an upstairs window; a curtain twitched.

"Shhhhh," said Lily, pressing herself to the ground.

"Hey," said Snake, "it's a speech impediment. There's no need to mock."

"I wasn't—Oh, forget it," said Lily. "Right. Mole, you're good in the dark. Are you coming with me into the cellar?" She hoped so. She felt woefully unprepared to go into the house again, frightened by the shadows moving behind the curtains and the deep darkness of the hole.

"Will there be spiders?" said Mole. "I don't like spiders."

"Very probably," said Lily, who was afraid of a lot of things, but not spiders.

"Oh, well. Still. It will be an honor, yes!" Mole pattered over to the hole. "After me!" she said, and tumbled in, head-first.

There was a very brief rushing sound, of fur against brick, followed by:

"Ow."

"Everything all right?" said Lily.

"Oh, yes. There's a bit of a drop to the cellar floor, it turns out. Gosh! I can see stars! I can see!"

Lily grimaced and followed.

Feetfirst.

16

Things went quite well this time. To begin with.
Lily landed hard, on her feet and then her bottom, and the breath was knocked out of her.

She drew in air, and she immediately felt something sharp dig in to the skin of her leg, and reached under her. Her fingers closed on an object, which she lifted up in the gloom.

It was an old key, rusted, with a sort of heart shape on the end that you'd loop chain or string through and a long toothed bit to go into the barrel of a lock. Large and blackened by age. She'd never seen it in the cellar, so it must have been in the coal chute, and she'd swept it down with her.

Shrugging, she slid the key into the back pocket of her jeans.

"Are you all right?" said Mole.

"Just about," said Lily.

Then she picked up Mole, dazed still, and tucked the round, furry creature under her arm. She looked around in the murky half-light. She hadn't been down in the cellar many times, but she had been here a couple of months ago, to help her mum sort out old baby clothes of hers and see what to keep for the new baby. At least, that had been the idea. Lily had sat on one of the big plastic bags of onesies and bibs and sulked instead.

Now she knew she had to be careful not to trip over an old broken stroller or a high chair or a tricycle or whatever else her real parents kept down here. She didn't want to make any noise—if the parent-things got her again, she might not escape so easily this time. There was a light bulb above the simple, rough wooden staircase, but she didn't dare pull the string to turn it on.

Gingerly, making as little sound as possible, she made her way to the stairs, then edged up. At the top the door opened into the hallway that led from the entryway in front to the new kitchen. She was getting tired now. Her energy didn't last long in the best of times, and this had been a long night. She knew she'd pay for it the next day. She'd be shivery and sick and have to lie down a lot.

If there was a next day.

Holding her breath, she eased the door open. The hall was empty. She heard footsteps on the floorboards above. Then another set. The things were upstairs.

She tiptoed along, past the door to the dining room, and then she was at the kitchen door, which hung open.

So easy.

Lily went in. There was the big new L-shaped countertop, an island next to it, three big lamps hanging above. Not lit, of course. Past the island was the wide, long oak table they'd had for years and a much newer sofa. Her mum had always wanted a sofa in the kitchen.

The note wasn't on the sofa, though. It wasn't on the side counter either, where her parents kept keys and scribbled shopping lists.

Lily went to the table, where she felt sure it would be—but there was nothing. Feeling a little frantic now, she moved a shopping bag that had been left on its side, a chocolate bar spilling out—

And there it was. Her granny must have covered it by accident.

Lily floated her hand over to it, almost not believing it. She was there. She'd pictured this in her mind: lifting the note, reading what it said.

"What's happening?" whispered Mole.

"We're in the kitchen," she said. "I've found the note." In her mind this meant everything was going to be okay. She could get out of this nightmarish loop of breaking into her own house with small animals as her accomplices.

"Oh! What does it say?"

"I don't know," said Lily. "It's a bit dark."

"Welcome to my world," said Mole. "Aren't we a pair!"

"Shhh," said Lily.

"Sorry."

Lily walked over to the big bifold doors, where faint light spilled through from the moon and stars above the garden. She peered down at the note. The night was dripping away, slowly, like water leaking out of a bucket, and soon her parents might be home, to a house full of demons.

Little Sadler!

Her parents were in a hospital in the next town, in something called a Midwife-Led Unit. They could practically have left the car at home and walked. Though her mum probably hadn't been in the mood for walking, Lily thought. She'd not liked it that much even at Christmas, and she was bigger now than then.

There was a phone number on the note and an address on the main road. Lily knew one thing about main roads, and that was that they were easy to find. She grinned. She'd get her bike—yes, her bike! From the shed. And she'd be there in less than an hour, if she cycled fast.

Behind her the door creaked, once, and then opened.

"Again?" said her mother's voice.

Lily turned, heart thudding in her chest, Mole clutched tight to her side. Her father was standing there too.

"Dispose of her," said Lily's mother. "And make it more permanent this time."

17

Lily ran skittishly over the smooth wooden floor and, once her hand was able to close on the slippery handle, tried the bifold doors with a yank, but they were locked.

"Mole!" she said. "Help! What do I do?"

"The mole can't help you," said the father-thing. "It's just a manifestation of your subconscious."

Lily could feel the warm mass of the mole in her hands. "No, she's not," she said.

"Still can't help you," said the father-thing.

He grinned—and ran at her.

Turning, panicking, still clutching Mole, Lily ran the other way, toward the father-thing, zigging down one side of the kitchen island as he zagged down the other side. She caught the edge of the countertop as she rounded the end, past the fridge, and her elbow rang out with a bell toll of pain, but the door was only there, in front of her, if she could just get past her mother.

She feinted right, then dived left past the mother-thing, and she was in the hall, but her dad must have pivoted fast on his feet because she heard the thud of his boots behind her and then came weightlessness, his arms under hers, lifting her off the ground.

But Lily had a trick for that, something the demons wouldn't know about, like they didn't know not to call each other "honey" or that her father was partly deaf. It was a thing she'd done when her parents had tried to lift her out of a bath when she was little—a thing of going floppy all over, making her whole body droop down, so there was nothing to get a purchase on.

She did that now, sliding down and out of his hands, dropping Mole just for a second and scooping her up again, and then she crawled through the dad-thing's legs and ran, turning to go up the stairs.

Two stairs at a time—*bam, bam, bam*—her pulse racing and breath coming ragged. At the top she turned left, then right, and made for her room, where there was a cupboard—you opened the door and it looked like there were just dresses and tops and suits hanging from a rail, shelves stacked with towels next to them, but actually, there was a space behind all that, for the water heater and some kind of pressure contraption for more powerful showers, and next to *that* there was another space, a cavity, just big enough for a little girl.

She ran past her bed, grabbing Willo along the way and shoving the stuffed whale up her top, since she was already holding a mole, before flinging open the door to the cupboard.

She threw herself in, past the clothes, and pulled the door behind her as much as she could, darkness following her into the cupboard—and then she was squeezing painfully through the copper pipes leading into and out of the big round tanks. And then she was in the little space, hidden by the piles of towels, the hanging clothes.

"Are we hiding?" whispered Mole. Lily was still clutching her under her arm.

"Yes," said Lily under her breath. She was fighting to control it, her breath, fighting not to pant, to let the air come quietly into her lungs and out again.

Heavy tread of boots in the room outside. Her dad

always wore boots. He was an architect and was often at building sites. Her real dad wouldn't wear them inside, of course. But this wasn't her real dad.

The cupboard door opened with a creak, and a widening crack of light appeared, a bright gap in the world.

Lily shrank back into the corner.

The dresses moved, swished. The father-thing was feeling among them, as if Lily might be standing there, posing as an outfit.

She held her breath.

Then, suddenly, a hand appeared, between two towels, fingers exploring, reaching.

Lily curled herself even farther back; she wasn't sure how much longer she could hold her breath. It was warm in here, from the hot-water tank, and dusty, too—the space where the pipes were had not been dusted in forever, and there was thick, gray, soft stuff everywhere, getting into her nose, getting into her airways, and—

Oh no.

Oh no, the hand was still there, pushing through the towels, messing them up, searching, and soon he'd realize there was empty space behind them. Again it struck Lily that he didn't know all the things her real father knew, he

was a hollow man, standing in her dad's stead. Her father would have yanked the towels aside right way, to reveal the space behind them.

It was a tiny thing . . .

But, no, it didn't matter, it didn't help—because Lily was going to sneeze.

Desperately, she tried to push it down inside her, hold the explosion at bay, but it was no good, it was coming, it was coming—

The father-thing's fingers stopped, as if they knew, as if they sensed the coming cataclysm.

And then she felt a clawed hand over her mouth, or a paw, whatever it was called on a mole, pinching the skin between her lip and her nose, and suddenly, miraculously, the sneeze eased its grip—and then was gone.

The hand disappeared, the towels settled, and the door shushed closed again. Darkness washed over Lily and Mole.

"Has he gone?" said Mole quietly.

Lily didn't dare answer.

The footsteps receded. He was leaving the room.

She was safe. She had stayed hidden.

She let out her breath, then sucked air in greedily. Beautiful, beautiful, dusty, smelly air. Amazing.

And then she heard the footsteps return, and the door opened, and the hand swept the dresses aside, the shirts, the skirts, and her dad crouched down, face appearing suddenly, like when you walk along a street at night and the moon appears in an instant from behind a house you're passing. He smiled sickly at her.

"Got you," he said. "I knew you were there all along. Just messing with you. Hide-and-seek. Fun! I'm sure your real dad pretended for years that he didn't know where you were. But parents always know. It's their job to keep you safe, after all." He paused. "Not mine, though."

18

The father-thing reached in and grabbed Lily, dragging her out of the cupboard.

She kicked and thrashed and writhed, but he was a moving statue; he didn't even grunt. She tried the going-slack trick again, but it didn't work this time. He just tightened his grip, burning rings on her limbs, and carried her to the landing, then down the stairs.

In the hallway, that was when Mole wriggled out from under Lily's arm and fell to the flagstone floor before clatter-sliding along, pulling herself with her big clawed hands, her black fur glossy against the ground, making for the kitchen. She looked purposeful, and Lily wondered for a moment what she was doing. But not for a long moment.

"Mother," said the father-thing.

The mother-thing stepped out from behind the kitchen door and stopped, regarding Mole, who was continuing to scrape along. The father-thing had also stopped and was watching, holding Lily.

"Mole!" shouted Lily. "She's in front of you!"

Mole, of course, couldn't see. She slid down the shallow step from the hallway to the smooth new wooden floor of the kitchen, and the mother-thing angled down and scooped her up in a seamless movement and held Mole in a fist, like a clump of rags.

Lily looked up at the father-thing. He was smiling slightly. She reared back her head, then flung it forward, biting at his shoulder, bringing her teeth together savagely. It did not yield, though, as flesh would. It was hard and cold and it hurt her teeth.

He cricked his neck and sighed. "Stop struggling, or the mole dies."

"And this is our domain now," said the mother-thing, holding up Mole. She gestured behind her with her other hand. "And your mole is in my hand. Look how small it is, how delicate. How easily it will snap, if I apply enough force."

"Doesn't everything?" said Lily, her voice coming out more confident than she felt.

"Not forever," said the father-thing. "We have the power to make you unbreakable, if you should want it. So be a good girl and stay still."

Mole squirmed to say something—to agree or disagree—but the mother-thing's grip was too strong, and she couldn't.

Why don't you just do it, then? Lily wanted to say to the parent-things, though she wasn't stupid enough to do it. *Why don't you just kill Mole?*

She watched them, their still heads and eyes.

Because they don't want to, was the only and obvious answer. *For some reason they don't want to.*

Lily didn't know what that meant, but she knew it meant something, and she stored it away.

"Are you going to be still?" said the father-thing.

Lily nodded. She was scared, for Mole. She didn't want Mole to be hurt.

He held her like she was a mannequin being moved in a store and went to the cellar door, which he kicked open. The stairwell yawned darkly.

"What are you—"

But he wasn't listening; he plunged down the stairs, and her head banged the wall as he clomped down to the old stone-floored cellar. Oh, she'd been wrong—they did want to kill her; she was going to die down here, he was going to kill her, he really was, and she'd never see her real mum and dad again, or even the new baby. There was a tiny part of her that had been curious to know what it might look like, a really, really tiny part, which she barely even admitted to herself.

And now—

Lily wondered how he was going to do it, her mind turning over the things down here in the cellar. A hammer? A box cutter? Her stomach squirmed with the horror of it. She flailed her head, butting him with the back of her skull, but he didn't even pause.

He stopped in front of the big metal shelving unit against the side wall, a simple steel frame bolted together. Shifting her weight to one arm, he pulled something down, a large object, rectangular, boxlike, and—

It was Buster's pet carrier—thick plastic with a handle on top and a metal-barred door that hinged and locked, the bars wrapped in squidgy plastic, only the lock had broken long ago, so now it had to be tied closed with string.

Buster howled and whined every time he had to go in there for a visit to the vet, scratching at the base of the carrier with his claws, his voice going high-pitched with distress. Lily had always felt sorry for him. Now, as she realized what was happening, as the father-thing crouched down and flicked open the door, she thought she would never let Buster go in it again because—

With a rough twist of her limbs and a sharp shudder that ran right up her spine to her teeth, as she hit the floor and then was pushed forward, she was propelled headfirst into the carrier, Willo squashed into her stomach. Surely she wouldn't fit in there, but then she was smaller than she'd ever been, the illness chipping her body from her bit by bit, as if telling her she was taking up too much space.

And then her dad pushed her legs in after her, like he was shoving laundry into a washing machine, and she curled up, she had to, and he closed the door and tied the string.

Apparently without effort, he lifted the dog carrier, with her in it, and put it back on the shelf. Lily twisted herself around, neck aching, so she could see his chest and stomach as he stood for a moment in front of the shelves.

"Stay quiet," he said. "Only breathe. Or you won't be breathing for long."

"W-why . . . ," she whispered. "Why are you locking me up? She said to do something permanent."

Brilliant question, Lily, she thought. *Just brilliant. What are you thinking?*

His head lowered, so that his coal eyes were looking into hers. "You were locked out," he said. "Usually that's us. Now, hush. Till I think of what to do with you."

He turned and walked away, and she heard his boots on the stairs, then the door closed, and there was inky darkness and silence.

A few moments passed, and then the stairwell yawned to life again, an opening mouth of light, and the father-thing came down— *clomp, clomp, clomp*—and Lily thought he might have decided to kill her after all, or maybe let her out, which was preferable but seemed less likely. He untied the string and opened the hinged and barred door. But then he shoved something in with her, something dark

and warm and whimpering, wriggling up so its furry body was next to Lily's face.

Mole.

Then he shut the door again and went back up the stairs, and the light followed him until it was gone.

"Well," said Mole, "this is cozy."

19

Till I think of what to do with you, the father-thing had said.

That was bad. Because what could possibly happen? What were his options, really—or hers?

Lily tried to push against the fastening but found that it was held firm with the string. She whimpered softly to herself.

If she began to starve in the pet carrier, she'd probably scream—she wouldn't be able to help herself—and the mother-thing would hear and come down here and that would be that. If her parents came back, like the mother had said, and got sick, she would still be down here, and then what? Even if the mother-thing didn't find out where she was, Lily would just run out of energy, would run down like a forgotten toy with fading batteries, and her mum and dad and The Baby would die, and she would be dead too, and . . .

No.

No, she wanted to live.

She thought of going to the hospital, the needles, the hours of boredom. Yes, even that she wanted. Because sometimes there was light that shafted through the windows; sometimes someone left one of those windows open a crack and she smelled wind and trees.

"What do we do?" she said to Mole, who was squashed up by her head, scrabbling with her paws.

"Are we in a hole?" Mole answered. "Could I dig? I'm trying, but the surface is hard and slippery."

"No," said Lily. "We're in a box." She was starting to become accustomed to the dark now—she could make out the objects in the cellar: an old bike, boxes. Dim light was filtering down through the coal chute they had opened.

"Oh. It's very smooth."

"Plastic."

Mole gave a little sigh. "I don't think I can get through it. My claws just slide off."

"Thanks for trying," said Lily.

Her shoulder was hurting, her right thigh, too—nearly

cramping, actually. She winced with pain and tried to push her foot against the bars, but there was no space, no room to maneuver, and there was something pointed and hard pressing into her backside. She was folded in on herself and she was in a box and oh no—this was panic; panic was coming—she was breathing very fast, sweat on her forehead, trickling down past her eyes, everything constricting so that the whole world seemed contained between these little plastic walls she was squashed up inside of and—

A swish, a surprised cry, and a small thud.

"Ouch."

Then an even smaller thud.

"Ow," said a second voice, tiny and high.

"Ugh," said the first voice. "Underground. It's not natural. Wings are made for air."

"Stop complaining," said the second. "Let's find Lily! And rescue her! I don't have my sword anymore, but I'm sure I can improvise." A pause. "Look! Nails! Rusty ones! That's iron. I can stab them with one of those."

"Maybe you can," said the first voice, raspier, more authoritative. "But as you said, we need to find Lily first."

Crow.

Crow and Mouse.

"I'm here," said Lily. "So's Mole."

Her view was a barred window, small, upside down. After a moment she heard two feet and four paws patter over to the ground below, just out of sight.

"You're in that little box up there?" said Crow.

"Yes."

"Doesn't seem very smart. How are you going to get your note like that?"

"I'm not in here *deliberately*," said Lily. "And I found the note. But then the . . . the parent-things found me. And Mole. They were going to do something to Mole if I didn't stop struggling. And I did struggle! Though it wasn't making much difference, actually. And, um, I stopped. Because of Mole. Because they were going to hurt Mole."

She was babbling. She should stop babbling. She was ill—she didn't have to justify not having defeated the parent-things. Strangely, though, she felt like she did.

"Oh," said Mouse. "We wondered. Why it was taking so long. And then Crow saw you running from those things in the kitchen. That's why we came down the coal chute after you. You should have defeated them. That's what you're supposed to do."

Which didn't make her feel better.

"Thanks," said Lily icily. "I'll try that next time." She would, though, maybe, joking aside. She wasn't scared anymore—she was really, really furious. When the mother-thing had squeezed Mole . . . That had stirred something inside her, something that had been lying at the bottom of her, invisible, like silt that rises up at the edge of a clear lake when you step into it.

"Can you get out?" said Crow. "Of that basket thing?"

"Obviously not," said Lily in her best withering tone, which wasn't very withering. Her chest and voice box were really quite constricted. "Could you two get us out of here, please? Mole's claws don't work on plastic."

"It's quite homey, though," said Mole. "Reminds me of a tunnel."

"Ignore Mole," said Lily. "Get me out now. Now, now, now. Everything hurts and I'm . . . I'm . . ." *Scared*, she wanted to say. *Panicking*. Only she felt a bit less scared now that the other animals were here. And there was something swirled in with the fear now too, like mixing paint. Anger.

"All right, all right, just let us think," said Crow.

"Sssssssoooo," said a third voice. "What'ssss Lily doing in that box?"

20

A little higher," said Mouse. "Nearly . . ."

Crow was hovering, just below the steel shelf, Mouse held in his claws. Lily could just see his wings, beating, from her twisted, upside-down vantage point.

"Slightly forward," instructed Mouse.

"I can see that, thank you," said Crow, a little out of breath, his wings whirring. One of them beat the air elegantly; the other was hunched, so that he hung there slightly lopsided, as if only one side of him remembered how to be lighter than air.

"It's not you who's going to fall if we get it wrong," said Mouse.

There was only a narrow ledge of shelf in front of the

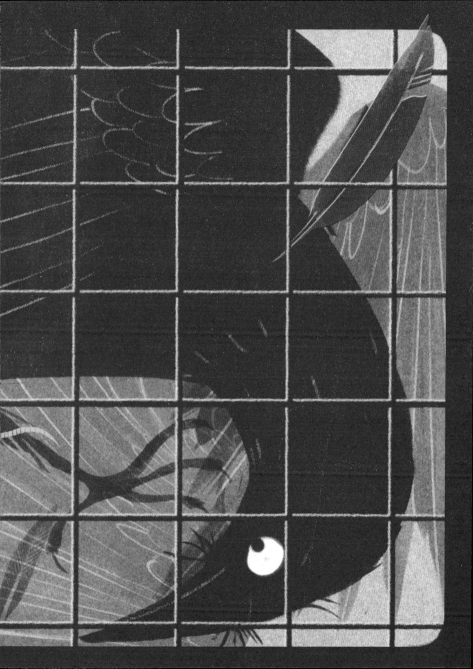

carrier for him to land on—a tiny mistake, and he'd hit the stone floor five feet below.

"Ssssh," said Snake, invisible to Lily, from below. "You both fell down the coal chute and that was higher."

"That was different," said Mouse. "I landed on Crow. He's surprisingly bouncy."

"What's happening?" asked Mole from where she was pressed against Lily's face.

"It's . . . hard to describe," said Lily accurately.

Wings going like mad, Crow had Mouse suspended just above the small strip of shelf now, and he opened his claws without warning. Mouse dropped with a small metallic bang. He clung on.

"Bull's-eye!" he said.

"Bull? Where?" said Mole.

Lily breathed deep, trying to remain calm, even as she was curled over herself like a folded piece of paper. "Okay," she said to Mouse. "Can you nibble through?"

She could see the string, where the father-thing had tied it, old and worn and stained but holding the door shut very firmly.

Mouse sniffed at the string while Crow flew over to an old scooter and perched on the handlebars. Then Mouse began to bite, paws securing the string as he gnawed.

Moments later the string fell apart.

Without thinking, desperate for space, desperate for air, Lily kicked out, and the door swung open hard, flinging Mouse far across the cellar, where he hit a pile of wine boxes.

"Oh no!" said Lily as she worked her way out of the box. "Oh no, I'm so sorry."

Mouse gave a little cough. "S'all right," he said, dusting himself off. "I'm mighty, remember?"

Lily moved clumsily, squirming legs first, backward, until her belly was over the edge of the ledge, then she let herself drop to her feet. Instantly, one of those feet melted into a shivering, shimmering mass of pins and needles, and she went down on a knee with a gasp. She held her breath as the excruciating, exquisitely excruciating feeling passed, like something draining out of her leg.

Tentatively, she put her weight back on her foot. It held. Just.

She stood.

"Right," she said, looking at her little army of animals. "Now I'm mad." She thought of Mole, how deflated and weak she had looked, how raglike, in the mother-thing's hand. She thought of all the animals and how they would die if the parent-things were allowed to stay in the house, where the well was, not just her animals, but *anything* magical that depended on the old waters. "And I want those things out of here."

"Good," said Crow. "Time to act."

"Time to take the fight to them!" said Mouse, raising a fist.

"But . . . how?" Lily said. "What can I do against them?"

"The ansssswer is inside you," said Snake.

"You said that before," said Lily. "I mean, not *you*. But one of you. Only, I don't know what it means."

All of the animals were silent. Still and silent and as useless as stone. They looked at her blankly.

"Wait," she said. "Do you . . . do you guys not know what it means either?" she asked.

"No," said Crow, shaking his head. "We only know what we said. Animals are like that."

Lily kicked furiously at the steel shelving. That was a mistake because it set off another frisson of pins and needles, an aftershock reverberating up her foot and shin.

Wait.

Steel.

Steel . . . and iron.

She remembered holding that horseshoe, the one the animals said had to go back up, to protect the house. Remembered its meaningless map of rust, the contour lines and bursting stars of it. The weight, in her hands.

Then she remembered the feeling, in the pet carrier, of something pressing into her skin, and she put her hand in her back jeans pocket and found the key, the old ornate key that she had disturbed when she came down the coal chute.

She took it out and held it up in the half-light, which was dotted with slow-turning motes of dust, from the chute.

A key.

She thought of the lock on the front door, the one they never used, the ancient one, because they'd never found a key for it.

A key. A lock.

An *iron* key.

"What's she doing?" said Mole.

"Lost her mind, it looks like," said Mouse.

"Oh, shame," said Mole.

"No," said Lily. She turned to them. "Iron. They don't like it, right? It stops them getting in to places?" She was picturing the horseshoe; the iron grille over the chimney.

"Oh, yes," said Crow. "They hate it."

"Iron like this?" She held the key in front of Crow. "I think it locks the front door. I found it when we slid down here. I'm wondering . . . maybe I was *meant* to find it. It's very old."

"I like the way you're thinking," said Crow.

"Righto, then," said Mouse. "So what are you going to do?"

"I'm going to go upstairs," said Lily. "And I'm going to make those things leave, and then I'm going to lock them out."

21

She started up the stairs.

"That's great," said Mole. "But could you carry me? I'm not so good with stairs."

Lily stopped. "Oh, yes. Sorry. Of course." Though it was ruining the drama of her moment a bit. She went back to Mole, put the key in her front pocket, then picked up the warm, round animal and placed her in the hood of her sweatshirt so she could keep both hands free.

"I mean," said Crow as they climbed the stairs—or, rather, as Lily climbed and he hopped behind her—"it's not *quite* the plan I was expecting."

"No?"

"No. I thought you might . . . procure a weapon or

something. A sword. Swords are conventional."

"A key is a kind of weapon," said Lily. "It bars entry."

"Not a weapon," said Crow. "No one ever turned up at a battle and said, 'Don't worry, chaps, I've got an old rusty key.'"

"All right, fair enough. But it's worth a try."

"Huzzah!" said Mouse, from where he was scurrying along a step. "Courage! Fortitude! Bravery!"

"Courage and bravery are the same thing," said Crow.

"No, they're not," said Mouse.

"Yes, they are."

"Oh, really? So why would they be two different wor—"

"Ssssh," said Snake.

They had reached the top of the cellar stairs. The door was open a crack. No sound came from the hall beyond it. Lily stood with her hand on the handle for one, two, three seconds—or maybe not seconds; she was timing with the beat of her heart. No one made a noise.

Eventually, she eased the door open and stepped out into the hall. Various small animals stood with her, a little menagerie. Lily was aware of how ridiculous they all must look, her and the crow and the mouse and the mole and the snake, silhouetted by the moonlight. Ridiculous and weak.

She shivered.

No.

No—she had iron, right at her hand. She instinctively reached for the key in her pocket, squeezed it and felt its shape imprint against her palm. But where were the parent-things? Where would such creatures go? She had to find them, now.

"Where do your parents spend most of their time?" whispered Crow.

"Why?"

"That's where they'll be," he said, as if reading her mind. "Drawing energy."

"Watching TV on the sofa, I suppose," said Lily. In her mind was an image of her and her parents, in front of *Britain's Got Talent* with take-out pizza, all warm and safe and together.

"Where?"

"Through that door there."

She pointed to the door to the living room. It was old and white and chipped, with a big black iron lock assembly a little like the one on the front door, held by ancient screws, with a hole for an old-fashioned key and a round brass handle, worn smooth by hundreds of years of hands, almost glowing in the pale light.

It was also shut.

"Is it locked?" said Crow.

"No," said Lily.

"They might be in there, then," he said. "They couldn't get through a door that was locked with an iron bolt."

Good, thought Lily. She was feeling better and better about her plan with the iron key. Though not good, because she also had to be brave enough to open the living room door. She reached out for the handle and oh so slowly turned it. Then—the light creak of it seeming very loud—she swung the door open.

They all peered inside. The living room was empty.

"Anywhere else?" said Mouse.

"Their bedroom, maybe," said Lily. "Mum's been spending a lot of time in bed. She had morning sickness, and now she has something called pre-ecla . . . Um, pre-thingamabob. It makes her tired." Lily had felt angry about her mum being shut away, frustrated at being left alone to do her homework or play with her toys while her mum lay resting in bed, but now, for the first time, she felt a pang of pity. She wouldn't want to be stuck in the bedroom, watching daytime TV.

A pang of pity—and a bolt, like lightning fizzing through her, of missing her mother.

Anyway, the bedroom was where her mum had spent a lot of time lately, and her dad, too, ferrying her cups of tea and plain cheese sandwiches, which was pretty much all she ate.

"Where?" said Mouse.

"Upstairs," said Crow. "It's where the mother caught us when we came down the chimney. Right?"

"Right."

So Lily moved Mole from her hood to her chest, hugged her briefly, tightly, soaking in her warmth, and then cautiously, trying not to creak on the wooden floorboards, they climbed the stairs. When they came to the bedroom, the door was open. Lily took one long, deep breath, her whole body vibrating like a tuning fork, then she walked in.

Crow, perhaps surprised by her lack of hesitation, flapped awkwardly through behind her and landed on the curtain rail with a clumsy fluster of wings. The parent-things were on the bed, sitting still next to each other, the mother holding the baby, and they turned to Crow first, heads moving like machinery, a simple twist from one position to another.

Then they turned to Lily.

Tick, tick.

"I am really very bored of this now," said the mother-thing. Then she turned to Lily's pretend dad. "You were meant to dispose of her."

"I did."

She stood, in one hinging, inhuman motion. "Clearly not. Kill her—now."

The dad-thing turned toward her.

"You'll have to catch me first," said Lily, taking a step backward.

She had only one half-formed plan in her mind: make them chase her outside through the front door somehow, so that she could then double back inside again and lock them out with the iron key.

Assuming, of course, that it actually *was* the key to the old lock.

And that she could somehow get *both* of them outside, at the same time.

The father-thing sprang into motion, toward Lily, and

Lily turned awkwardly, banging her shin on the radiator as she threw herself through the doorway and out onto the landing, Crow flapping panicked above her and the other animals tumbling down the stairs.

This was—it was rapidly becoming clear to her—not a very good plan.

22

Out in the hallway, at the top of the stairs, something made Lily pause: a flicker of colored light in the corner of her vision, even though Mouse was already at the bottom of the stairs, even though the father-thing was right behind her, even though she could hear the air moving as he reached out.

She grabbed the courage bead necklace that had caught her eye from the bowl in which it sat, coiled. It was tied at only one end since she'd still been adding beads to it; and she flung it behind her now as she took the stairs two at a time, one hand on the bannister. She heard the beads clattering to the floor and then a complicated sliding sound—

A literally inhuman scream—

And then the father-thing was tumbling, head over heels

down the stairs, beads pinging down after him—*ping, ping, ping*—and then he was landing on his head, twisted grotesquely, legs and feet up in the air above his snapped neck.

He didn't move.

He didn't move, and Lily made the mistake of standing there, staring, thinking, *Is he dead? Can* they *die?*

He wasn't, or he was already, or dead didn't really mean anything with something like him, because he stood, cricked his neck with an audible click, and rotated his head on it, as if after a stressful day.

"That hurt," he said, looking at her with his coal eyes, duller and harder than ever.

She turned and ran, clutching Mole tight.

She could hear the father-thing just behind her, getting closer.

Lily ran down the hall, catching her arm and scratching it on the little nails in the coatrack that her parents used for hanging scarves and hats. But she didn't cry out. She kept running down the hall toward the new kitchen, remembering Crow telling her to find a weapon, the father-thing's footsteps behind her, and then she rounded the island.

She yanked open the drawer of the farthest cabinet unit, turning to face him as he entered the kitchen.

"Nowhere left to run," he said. "I should have finished this in the cellar."

She scrambled blindly with her left hand, searching for something, anything, and she came out with a meat tenderizing hammer.

She held it in front of her, like a person holding a cross in a vampire movie.

"What are you going to do with—" he began, but she went for the surprise factor, flinging herself forward, the hammer whirling, striking a glancing blow on his shoulder; she swung it back again, then forward, curving to his head, but he got a hand up, and crunch went the hand.

Angry now, he grabbed her wrist with his good hand, hard, and forced her back against the island. Pushing. Pushing. A barstool leaned away from her, then fell with a glassy rattle. Her back was against the cold countertop.

His glittering black eyes were on hers. Very deliberately, he brought down her hand that held the hammer, once, again, again, again on the countertop, smashing it over and over, until she screamed and opened her hand and the meat hammer fell out with a disappointing, small clunk. Now she was unarmed.

All this happened very fast, and Mole surged up through Lily's arms and clawed at the father-thing's face. He staggered back, something like blood, but black, dripping from his eyes and cheeks.

Mole dropped to the ground and ran at him, clinging to his calf. "The well's right under our feet," she said. "I can feel it. It makes us stronger too."

And then Mouse was suddenly there, in the corner of Lily's vision, and he was up on the father-thing's shoulder and biting, biting at his ear, stabbing him with a rusty nail, which must have been iron because the father-thing was yelping, swatting at the little biting thing, and in some dim part of her mind Lily thought, *Oh, Mouse is really mighty after all.*

But—and this was still all so fast, this was all in seconds, in the tiniest of heartbeats, a mouse's heartbeat—the father pulled at Mouse and held him tight and flung him across the room. Then he lashed out with his foot, and Mole went flying, hitting the window and sliding down it with a small squeak.

"Stronger, but still small," the father said. "Still weak in the end." He turned to Lily. "Like you."

He walked over to her. He was so tall and so strong, and she was so small. She felt so small. She glanced at Mole, who was very still.

The father-thing pulled her close to him.

She closed her eyes.

And he drew back, hissing. He clutched at his hip.

She glanced down, confused. Hoodie. Jeans. Pocket.

The key.

Reaching into her jeans pocket, she took out the old key and held it out in front of her.

The father-thing backed away, eyes on it. Black eyes, no longer glittering. Just watching. Watching.

"Get. Out. Of. My. House," Lily commanded.

The father-thing snarled. "You can't make me," he said.

"Oh, yes, I can," she said.

And he said nothing, so she knew she was right. She couldn't believe it could be so easy, so simple.

Keeping the key in front of her, she walked toward him, and he backed away all the time, down the hallway, past the door to the cellar where in another life she'd come up with the animals, and to the front door.

"Call the other one," Lily said, eyes never leaving him. "The one that looks like my mum."

"Yes!" said Mouse, who had climbed up Lily's body when she wasn't paying attention and was now standing on her shoulder. "Both of you, out!"

The father-thing sighed, then made a sound, a call, that

was like nothing Lily had ever heard—there was more of the wind in it, of rivers, of rain, than there was of voice. The mother-thing appeared at the top of the stairs and began to come down, quicker than Lily's real mother could, taking the stairs in a way that made it seem like her legs didn't bend in normal places.

"That's right," said Lily. "It's you who's leaving."

The mother-thing stood with the father-thing.

"Banish us if you like," said the mother-thing. "We'll get back in."

Lily thought of the horseshoe. She thought of her own illness, how it would never really leave her, not without a transplant, but it could be managed, with medication, with transfusions. Maybe the fake parents were a bit like a chronic illness. You couldn't necessarily kill them. But you could keep them at bay.

She smiled. She'd have to tell Dan the therapist about that one. She was sure he'd like it.

"No," she said to the mother-thing. "You won't get back in. Because I know how to keep you out. I know how to defeat you. I just need iron." She brandished the key.

Both parents hissed.

"Now out," said Lily.

The father-thing looked down at the door handle, the round knob set in the big iron housing.

"We can't," he said.

Still holding the key firm and high with one outstretched arm, Lily carefully reached past them with her free arm toward the front door, and as she did so, they tried their last, weak trick—the father-thing grabbing her so suddenly that she recoiled. But she wasn't scared anymore, and she didn't drop the key; instead, she swung it around and pushed it into his face, and he fell back, screaming like a storm outside a window.

She twisted the handle and opened the door. Then she stepped back, holding up the key.

"We'll just open the door again," said the mother-thing as the two of them slid outside.

"No, you won't," said Lily. And she slammed the door in their faces. Then she locked the lower lock that hadn't been used in decades. Centuries, maybe.

She leaned against the inside of the door and closed her eyes.

Then she fainted, slid down, and crumpled to the ground, lying on the coir welcome mat like a strange, forgotten parcel. But Lily didn't feel any of it.

23

Something wet.

Something wet was on her nose, on her cheek, ugh, it was gross, it was—

It was Mole, sitting on her chest, licking her face.

Lily sat up gently.

"You can stop that now," she said. "Um. Thanks. I think."

Mole nodded. "You could stand to wash your face occasionally," she said.

"Oh," said Lily, not sure whether to be offended. She didn't know if a mole not liking the taste of your skin was good or bad.

There was a sudden and sharp pain in her hand—she screamed and pulled it close, rubbing it with her other hand.

Mouse stood on the flagstone floor where her hand had been, a pair of nail scissors in his paw, which he had found who knows where.

"I was *awake*," said Lily. "I was *sitting up*."

"Just making sure," said Mouse. He looked down at the scissors. "I thought these would be cleaner than the nail."

"Oh, how thoughtful." Lily looked around. "Are they . . . ?"

"Gone?" said Crow. "Yes."

Over by the stairs Snake's head appeared, followed by the rest of his body. "Hate sssstairs," he said. "Ssssssssooo, what did I miss?"

"Lily locked them out! Mole licked her face! I stabbed her hand! But in a nice way." Mouse puffed up his chest proudly.

"Sssssounds dramatic," said Snake. He bared his needle teeth, in what might have been a smile. "What now?"

Lily stood. "I'm going to the hospital in Little Sadler. To find my parents." She could just call them, of course, from the landline. But she had to see them, her *real* parents. With her own eyes. To hold them and be held by them.

"Great. Let's go," said Crow.

"What, you're coming too?"

"Apparently."

"Apparently?"

"I rather think that when you no longer need us, we . . . won't be here anymore," said Crow. "So if we're still here, you still need us."

"Why would I still need you?"

"I don't know."

She sighed. "Wonderful. Okay. Let's go to the shed. Get my bike."

Before they did, though, Lily turned on the lights. Every one she came to: she flicked switches, and the hallway filled with light, from lamps and overhead fixtures. The stairwell lit up too, and the hallway above, even the little wall sconce at the bottom of the stairs.

"Good thinking," said Crow. "That'll help keep them away."

"*Help?*"

"You can't be too safe," said Mouse.

"Oh, great," said Lily, and tried not to think about it. She switched on the lights in the kitchen as they walked through—the three big curved ones hanging above the island, the floor lamp in the corner, the LED glow beneath the cabinets. Then she opened the bifold doors—the black expanses of glass sliding smoothly on their gliding mechanism—and they were back out in the garden.

Only then Lily hesitated. "Wait," she said. "Those things. They're out here."

Crow laughed—a screeching sound. "Outside?" he said. "Outside belongs to *us*."

"The earth," said Mole.

"The air," said Crow.

"All the small spaces between things," said Mouse.

Snake, Lily noticed, said nothing. But she felt better anyway. She stood there and let the cool air flow over her face. Darkness lay on the garden, as it had before, as if darkness was all there was and ever would be, and daylight was just a dream. But stars were shining, high in the sky. And the animals were with her, and they were confident, and that made her veins sing with life.

It was strange. She'd spent so long—hours—trying to get in, and now they were going out again. But the light from the house spilled onto the grass now, and the windows were bright too, and the house was alive again; occupied. Even if just by light. And she was going to see her parents, at the hospital, and everything was going to be as it was. Not as it was before the pregnancy, before her illness, which was what "before" had always meant to her until tonight.

No, not that anymore—just the time before those creatures came along and tried to take what she loved.

She went to the shed, closing the bifold doors behind her. The animals followed, Crow flitting from bush to bush. There was a padlock on the shed, but it was never locked; it just looked like it was. She opened the door and took her bike out from where it had been leaning against a wall. She'd gotten it for her birthday two years ago. It was a little small now, but it was bright yellow and blue, and it had a basket at the front and lights and the tires were pumped up.

"I'll put you in the basket," she said to Mole.

"Basket? Of what?" said Mole.

"It's best you don't know," said Crow.

"Oh, good, that inspires confidence," said Mole.

Lily lifted her gently in.

"Mouse," she said, "your turn in my hood, I guess?"

"I'll stay on your shoulder," said Mouse. "So I can see potential dangers ahead and warn you!"

"All right," said Lily, "but it might get a bit windy."

"That is of no consequence to me!" said Mouse.

"I will fly," said Crow. "I'm not going on that contraption."

"Contraption?" said Mole nervously.

Lily put on her helmet and walked the bike a little way down the garden path—she'd take the side way around the house, then follow their lane to the main street and along the A . . . well, it was the A something road. A193? She'd seen the sign a million times and couldn't remember. Anyway, she'd follow it to the hospital.

"Aren't you forgetting ssssmomething?" said a voice.

Lily looked down. There was Snake, on the path. She had almost forgotten him. And Lily also had an almost-thought then, something that nudged against her mind for attention. But she wasn't sure what it was; its shape, its outline, was soft and blurry. She shrugged it off and picked up Snake.

"I could sort of wear you, like a belt?" she said hesitantly. She was a little worried she might offend the still-quite-scary snake.

Snake gleamed green in the light from the house. "Fine," he said. His teeth showed.

"Don't bite me," said Lily.

"No," said Snake. "It's not time."

"What?"

"No. I mean no."

Lily pulled a face. But what could she do. She wound Snake around her waist, and he helped, and then he was on her, wrapped around her.

She turned on the bike lights, a white one for the front and a red one for the back. They were dim, but they were powered by a dynamo—when she pedaled, they'd get brighter. Once they passed the house, she turned the bike onto the road, swung herself over the saddle, and began to ride. The breeze pulled stray hairs out of her ponytail, whipping at her face. Their lane was long and poorly lit—she had to swerve by the vacant pub, to avoid broken glass, its windows black. Then she turned the corner onto the main street and shifted up a gear.

There was a tapping on her neck, insistent.

She squeezed the brakes—front and back, like her dad had always told her, so she wouldn't go over the handlebars—and stopped outside the sandwich shop.

She felt more than saw Mouse grab her ear with both little front paws.

"I'd like to go in your hood now, please," he said.

24

It must have taken at least an hour.

Crow flew ahead, once Lily told him where they were going, often landing in trees by the road and watching, beady-eyed, as they caught up. Lily wasn't used to cycling anymore, and her legs got tired, the muscles aching and on fire at the same time, as if they really wanted her to stop and were trying to tell her so in every way they knew.

She did stop, a few times, to catch her breath—once at the World War One memorial and then again, for longer, at the top of the main road, which was set on a hill. There, she leaned against a bus stop sign for some time before she felt ready to go on.

"We could take a bus," said Mouse, peeping out.

"I'm not going on the bus with a mouse, a mole, a

snake, and a crow," said Lily. "*Anyone* could be on a bus. Someone from school. I mean, it's late, but you never know. Or a teacher!" She was picturing it now. The questions. The weirdness. "Definitely not."

"Crow could fly alongside," said Mouse.

"That wouldn't make it better," said Lily.

"Fine," said Mouse with a little harrumph, before disappearing down inside her hood and curling up very small.

So Lily got back on the bike and started to pedal again. It was quite a busy road and only the first bit, before the speed limit picked up, had a sidewalk, so she went cautiously and slowly. Several times large trucks and SUVs went around her, wide, leaning on their horns.

"   ," said Crow whenever that happened, but fortunately, the wind snatched away his very rude words and whisked them down into the valley, to vanish.

It became a rhythm; a trance; a nightmare. The moon to Lily's left, the hedgerows flashing. The cars passing and their horns. The cold wind in her face. Mouse complaining.

But finally, they came to the next town, and Lily followed a wide curve down, then a road past the old woolen mill, its tower sticking up into the black sky, and onto the primary thoroughfare there. She was picking up her pace now; she zipped past a pedestrian crossing where the lights were green, and a drunk man shouted pointlessly at her.

And then there it was: a big lit-up building with a large parking lot that Lily felt sure must be the hospital. She hadn't known where it would be, but the town wasn't that big, and luckily, it was right there on the main street. Though it looked like it could have been a big sports hall or a school with lots of windows, she saw a sign on the side that read *MIDWIFE-LED UNIT*. There was even a taxi stand out front, with a couple cabs lined up in front of it. The door of one was open, the driver sitting with a leg out on the ground, smoking a cigarette.

Lily parked her bike, left the animals outside in a dark puddle of shadow beside a big garbage bin, and then followed the signs to the reception area, where there was a soda machine, a booth to pay for parking, and some sofas. There was one curving desk.

"Um, hello," she said to the woman sitting there behind a computer. The woman was young and had pink hair and a nose ring.

"Hello, love," she said to Lily. "Can I help you?"

"I'm looking for the Wilsons," said Lily. "My parents. They came to have a baby."

The woman peered at her. "Right. And . . . are you on your own?" She looked Lily up and down, and this gaze suddenly made Lily aware of how dirty she must be, how covered in dumpster dust and coal and mud.

"Yes. I mean, no. I was with my gran . . . er . . . she's in the car outside . . . and I wanted to see how things . . . were going." She paused, still conscious of the generally poor state of her appearance. "I fell over," she added lamely.

Lily didn't like how the woman was looking at her. "Right," the woman repeated, pushing her pink hair behind one ear. "And how old are you?"

Lily didn't see how this was relevant, so she didn't answer. "Can I see my parents?" she said.

The woman—her name tag said KATRINA—tapped on her computer screen.

"Oh," she said.

"Oh what?"

"They're in skiboo," said Katrina. Or at least that's what it sounded like.

"Ski . . . ?"

"Sorry," said Katrina. "SCBU. The Special Care Baby Unit. It's at the big hospital, in Wodebridge."

"But they came here."

"Yes. But then . . . Well, sometimes unexpected things happen. Nothing to worry about, I'm sure! But they have been transferred to Wodebridge General, where the doctors are. Um. Just to be safe, I imagine."

Lily slumped against the counter, fear and worry expanding again in her chest. A problem? With The Baby? With . . . her mum? She was ashamed to find she was hoping it was the baby. She didn't want to think about something happening to her mum. She didn't really want to think about hospitals at all. Especially not *her* hospital, the same hospital where she spent so much of her time. Actually, she didn't even think of it as her own time anymore—there was the hospital's time, the time that belonged to the doctors, which they took from her, and then there were the brief periods of respite they granted her, when she could pretend to have her own life.

But still. She was going to have to go there anyway.

Her parents needed her.

"Sorry," Katrina said again. "I'm sure they called your gran—maybe after you left the house . . . ?"

Lily nodded. Yes. That might have actually happened. But of course she'd left Granny Squeak's hours and hours ago. "I'd better get back to her, yes," she said a bit stiffly.

"All right," said Katrina. "I hope . . . I hope everything is fine. With . . . well, with everything."

"Thanks," said Lily. She turned, then turned back. "You don't have, like, a shopping bag I could borrow, do you?"

Katrina bit her lip, then rummaged under the desk and produced a Tesco bag. "Here you go, love," she said.

"Cheers," said Lily. It was what her parents often said. She was missing them more than she would have thought possible.

Outside she lifted Mole and Mouse into the bag, then Snake.

"I'm not going in that," said Crow.

"You have to," said Lily. "It's too far to fly with your injured wing."

"What's too far?"

"The hospital."

"Isn't this a hospital?"

"Not the right kind, apparently."

Crow ruffled his feathers, looking down in disgust. "This is a *shopping bag.*"

"Hush," said Lily. "They have security cameras. This must be looking weird already." She was conscious of a camera on a wall not far away. "Just get in, Crow."

Crow gave a sort of sigh-caw and hopped into the bag. The other animals made room for him.

"How are we going to get there, anyway?" said Mouse.

"We're going to take a taxi."

"Do you even know how to drive?" asked Crow.

Now it was Lily's turn to sigh. "We're not going to *steal* a taxi," she said. "We're going to get a ride in one."

"Yay!" said Mouse. "How exciting! Don't you need money for that?"

Lily closed her eyes and rubbed them, hard.

Oh no.

25

The first taxi was empty.

But in the second was a woman, large and smiley, with three different phones around her steering wheel, plugged in and glowing, trailing colored wires, showing maps and fares and things.

"Hello," she said when Lily tapped on the window. "Where are you going?"

"Wodebridge," said Lily. "The hospital."

"Aye. All right. It'll be about twenty pounds."

Lily cleared her throat. "Um. I don't have any money *right now*. But I'm going to find my parents. They'll have money. When we get there, I'll make sure you're paid."

The woman's smile had almost disappeared. "Your parents are at WG?"

"Yes. With The Baby. I mean, the new one. I don't know it yet."

"They've had a baby here? And now they've gone to the big hospital?"

"To the SC . . . something," said Lily.

"The SCBU," said the woman. "My niece was premature. Spent two months there. I ran the marathon for them once."

Lily was surprised, looking at her. It must have been a while ago.

"I know what you're thinking," said the woman. "But there's a lot of strength in this body." She slapped her leg. "I was a judo champion. But if you're going there, you ride for free. Hop in."

Yes, thought Lily, a sunrise of relief glowing within her, just an edge, on a horizon. She climbed into the taxi with her bag held carefully on her lap.

"That's not food, is it?" said the woman. "No eating in the taxi."

"No," said Lily.

"Debatable," said a very small voice from the bag. "Mouse lookssss quite tasssty."

"Hey!"

"What was that?" said the taxi driver, turning as they left the parking lot.

"Nothing," said Lily. "Just . . . humming to myself."

"Oh, I'm a singer myself," said the woman. She broke into a tuneless rendition of an Adele song.

Then another.

And another.

By the time they swung into the parking lot of Wodebridge General, Lily was sort of wishing she'd chosen a different taxi. But she was grateful, too, to have moved through space, to be closer to her parents.

"Thank you," she said as she got out.

"You're welcome," said the woman. "I hope the baby's all right."

Lily smiled at her through the window. "I hope so too," she said. As she said it, she realized it was true.

"Lovely voice," said Crow as they walked toward the entrance. "Reminded me of my mother."

"Nonsense," said Mole. "It made me wish it were my ears that didn't work, not my eyes."

26

L ily followed a long corridor with a red strip painted down the side wall. She knew the hospital well, had been here so many times, but not to this wing. A sign pointing to the left: *SCBU, ULTRASOUND, MRI.* She turned, following it.

Then another: *SCBU, ULTRASOUND*—through a big set of double doors.

There was no one around. She passed a bed on wheels, parked by the wall. She pushed through and down another corridor, then followed a sign marked *SCBU* to the right. It was like a maze of white-painted halls. There was some kind of squidgy black rubbery stuff running down the walls—bumpers, she realized, in case the wheely beds bashed against the sides when they were being moved.

Finally, she reached another glass double door, only this one had a security pad next to it, the numbers from 1 to 9 glowing green. There was a button and an intercom speaker.

Lily pressed the button and the speaker crackled.

"Hello?" said a man's voice.

"Oh, hi," she said. "My name is Lily Wilson. I'm here to see my, um, parents."

There was a pause while the crackle disappeared.

"Come in."

A buzz.

Lily pushed on the doors and they swung open, and her father was coming toward her. They were in a sort of air-lock corridor, more double doors ahead of them.

"Lily!" her dad said, and held his arms out wide. She found herself almost running, and then he was wrapping those arms around her, and she closed her eyes, breathing in the smell of him—deodorant and hair wax and something underneath it all that was just Dad.

"What are you doing here?" he said, stepping back. His eyes didn't have edges; they were real eyes, made to let in light. Happiness washed over her like the sea on holiday.

"I couldn't sleep. I rode my bike to the other place, and they said you were here." She was suddenly very conscious of the plastic bag in her hand with all the animals in it. She held it tight against her side.

"Oh," he said. Then he paused, disoriented. *"What?"* He looked at his watch. "How did you get here? Where's Granny?"

"She's at home. I took a taxi."

He stood there blinking for a moment. "Do I need to, er, pay the driver?"

"No," said Lily, brushing this off. "She was really kind."

"Right. Um. Good."

He seemed about to ask another question, so Lily spoke first, to stop him.

"I wanted to see you," she said. "Check that everything was okay. And . . . the baby."

Her dad's eyes widened. "Oh, yes. Would you like to meet your sister?" he said.

"Sister? I have a sister?" Complicated feelings turned in Lily's stomach.

"Yes. She's so perfect, Lily, you won't believe it. Just like you."

I'm not perfect, thought Lily. *I'm broken.* But she didn't say it.

"Does she have a name?" she said instead.

"Not yet. Your mum wanted to be a bit . . . surer. And to decide together."

He started to lead the way toward the double doors.

"What . . . I mean . . . Why did you have to come here? To the big hospital?"

He opened the doors. "She was having a bit of trouble breathing," he said. "The baby. So they need to keep her in here for a bit, check her out. They thought it might just be something-something distress of the newborn." He didn't actually say "something-something," but that was what Lily heard. "Or she might have a strep B infection." He frowned. "We're still not sure, but she's okay for now."

"Oh," said Lily. There was a feeling inside her of a bubble popping.

They had entered a wide, square room, with tall windows all down one end, only there was nothing but blackness beyond them at this time of night. In the corner was a nurse's station. And down each side of the room were plastic boxes, on legs, with babies in them. Wires and cables were going in and out of the boxes, attached to machines that whooshed up and down with air like an accordion or that beeped with flashing lights.

It was a place that spoke in bleeps—a language Lily understood.

They passed a woman who was breastfeeding a tiny baby, its hand connected to a drip by a tube, and then there, in the far corner, under the window, was Lily's mum, holding a bundle.

The bundle had a wire coming out of it and a thicker tube.

The bundle was a baby, wrapped in swaddling, a pink hospital blanket, but Lily could not make out its features from here. She stood for a second, unable to move, unable to approach. Shy, she realized. Which was an odd thing to be, in the presence of a tiny baby—something with so little power.

Her mum held out a hand. "Come, Lily," she said.

And so Lily did.

She drew near, and she saw a perfect face, asleep, tiny nose, a little rosebud mouth, and long eyelashes.

"Oh!" said Lily. "Oh, she's beautiful."

Her mum looked at her sleepily. There was strain around her eyes, written on her skin. "Hi, Lily," she said. "This is your baby sister. Yes. She's lovely, isn't she?"

It was a measure of how tired she must have been that

she didn't even seem to question what Lily was doing there.

There was a movement behind Lily, and she turned to see the nurse from the desk in the corner approaching. She was a smiling woman with a clipboard and short gray hair.

"You must be the older sister!" she said. She looked down at the board. "Well," she said to Lily's mum. "Chest X-rays are clear. We're just waiting on the blood tests to confirm the white cell count has come down. But"—she bent low and checked a machine that was hooked up to the baby—"stats and pulse rate are A-OK. So I'm happy with her vitals. You two could take a coffee break, if . . . um . . ." She looked at Lily.

"Lily."

"If Lily wants to hold the baby?"

Lily's mum and dad turned to her.

"Um," she said. Her chest was a box, and her heart was an animal in it, pitter-pattering. "Yeah. Yes. I would."

She put down the shopping bag carefully, under her mum's chair, trying to keep the handles folded down, so no one could see inside. She thought she heard a quiet squeak.

Her mum stood. She was wearing a long blue hospital gown, her own furry slippers underneath. "A coffee would be nice, actually," she said.

"There's a Caffè Nero in the atrium," said the nurse.

"Oh, we know it well," said Dad, smiling at Lily. "This one hid there once."

"I'm sorry?" said the nurse.

"Long story," he said.

Lily's mum sat Lily down, guiding her into the chair, and then she and the nurse handed the baby to her, together, easing her into Lily's arms, onto her lap, so that the wire wasn't disturbed, so that she wouldn't wake up.

"Okay," said Dad. "We'll see you in ten minutes. Fifteen."

"Er . . . on my own?" said Lily.

"We'll be here, love," said the nurse. "Nurses outnumber babies here, more or less."

"Okay," said Lily. She felt like there were lots of things she should be saying, but everyone was so tired, it didn't seem like the time, and words seemed heavy things to lift from the tongue.

She held the baby tightly and gently at the same time. She felt heavier than anything in the universe; she felt as light as air. She felt like she might float away, through the window, even though it was shut.

Lily looked at the little face, the chest moving up and

down. The eyelashes and the lips and the cheeks. She wanted to brush the tears from her own cheeks, but she couldn't lift her arms. She loved her little sister instantly and painfully. She couldn't believe the pain, but it was a good pain—it was a tearing, but like the earth tears to let a flower through, like a bud tearing to bring forth blossom.

"Hi," she said to the baby.

Her mum and dad were gone. The nurse effaced herself gracefully; she had experience with this sort of thing, of course, so she kind of moved backward and then was no longer there, was at her desk.

Lily stared down at her little sister's face for the longest time. She'd heard people say, in films and things, that they'd do anything for someone else, but she'd never understood it until this moment. The eyelashes. The nose. The softness of the skin. They made her think in a way she couldn't have put into words of tiny flowers in trees, in the spring, of clouds, of light held in the branched, thin skin of a leaf, of snow falling, of the sea's restless breath.

Then she looked up, and all the babies were gone, all the see-through plastic boxes with their cables, the machines, and the nurse and the nurse's station. The walls were blank, no posters anymore, she was just in a bare, white room. The windows were gone too. Blank walls, on all sides. There was no sound, either; all the beeping had stopped.

There was one door, where she had come in. Otherwise, the room had become the dog carrier, from before, only huge—even the walls didn't meet the floor at right angles, but were curved, like the plastic crate she'd been locked in, down in the basement.

She stood, holding the baby in her arms. There was no wire, no tube attached to her little sister anymore—they'd gone now, along with everything else. There was only a cot on wheels, in front of her, a smaller version of the bed she'd seen in the corridor.

Gently, she laid the baby in it. The baby stayed asleep.

Lily walked to the door and tried the handle. It was locked. There were two bolts, it looked like—she could see the screws and the housings—but she couldn't see any way of turning them, and the handle didn't move at all.

She had been locked out, almost the whole night, and now she was locked in.

27

L ily heard a rustle and turned.

The only other object in the white plastic room was an orange Tesco bag, and now it was lying on its side.

"Told you we were still needed," said Crow. He flew over and landed on her shoulder. Mole and Mouse sat on the floor.

"What's happening?" said Lily.

"We don't question, we just do," said Crow.

"Do what?"

"Whatever is needed."

"Which is?"

"I can't tell you that," he said.

"Well, *that's* helpful," muttered Lily.

She started to look around the room, the giant white dog carrier room, trying to find anything, any object, that might help her. But there was nothing: no windows, no keypads, no phones, just a smooth plastic box of a space, with her stuck in it, with her animals. And the baby, her baby, her sister, sleeping on that one cot.

"Help me look," she said to the animals.

"For what?" said Mouse.

"I don't know. Something. There must be something."

"Oh," said Mouse. "Right." He nosed off, sniffing, along the bottom of the wall. Lily expected some kind of follow-up question from him, but apparently, he was satisfied with his instructions.

"I can't look," said Mole. "So I'm just going to sit here."

"Um, okay," said Lily. She felt along the walls, circling the space, trying to see if there was anything she'd missed; but there wasn't.

"Wait," said Mouse. "There's something here."

Lily hurried over to where Mouse was sitting, just in front of the door. "What is it?" she asked.

"Some kind of . . . raised bit," said Mouse. "On the floor. Like a very low step or a plate or something."

Crow flew over and landed beside Mouse. "Oh, yes. I feel it with my talons." He was prodding at the floor with a clawed foot.

Lily squatted down. It was true: there was a kind of plate in the floor, square, and when she stood and stepped a foot on it, it made a gentle hissing sound and depressed slightly. Moved by her weight.

Weight.

She put both her feet on it, and it lowered farther. A pressure plate—was that it? She had to stand on it, to activate the locks, maybe?

She turned the door handle hopefully—

And nothing happened.

"What are you doing?" asked Crow.

"I think it's to do with weight," said Lily. "But it's not working."

"Perhaps you don't weigh enough on your own," said Crow.

"What do you mean?"

"I can't tell you."

"Stop saying that!" said Lily. "Stop saying you can't tell me!"

"Sorry."

Lily sighed. But then she looked over at the cot, and something occurred to her. She didn't weigh enough on her own. She went to the cot and picked up her baby sister, careful not to wake her, and carried her, snug in her arms, to the door. Then she stood on the pressure plate again.

Hiss.

Click.

One of the bolts slid open—Lily heard it and saw it, the metal bar disappearing into the door with a snick, so that the crack of light around the door grew larger.

But the other lock stayed where it was, and when Lily tried the handle, the door was still locked.

She could feel tears pricking at the corners of her eyes.

What was she supposed to do now? What was the point of all this? She had been outside nearly all night, scraping herself, hurting herself, terrified, locked out and locked in, and now she was trapped in a nightmare again, a blank white nightmare, and she couldn't think of anything that might help.

But then that thought nudged at her again, the one about the thing that hadn't been explained, the thing that wasn't of air, or earth, or the spaces between.

And then she saw the snake, slithering out of the bag, then along the wall to where she and Mouse and Crow were standing.

"You," she said to the snake.

"Me," he said.

She turned to Crow. "You all helped me," she said. "All of you helped. Crow, you got me in through the chimney. Mouse, you helped with the dog flap. And, Mole, you found the coal chute."

Mole nodded, solemn all of a sudden, solemn and slow.

"And, Mouse!" said Lily. "You gnawed through the string, and Crow carried you, and, and, and you all did stuff. But not Snake."

"No," said Snake.

Lily looked around at the white walls. "Did you do *this*?" she asked. "Did you . . . do something to the room?"

Snake kept his eyes on her. He didn't answer.

She looked now at his narrowing, sharp teeth. She thought of the needles, when the doctors sucked the blood out of her and injected things in her, of how she never wanted it, tried to run away, always resisted. How she'd hidden at Caffè Nero.

She thought of her therapist Dan, how he was always blabbering on about illness narratives and acceptance, and how she had to accept that she had a chronic illness that was unlikely to get better without some very lucky donor miracle, without a new kidney, without all those injections and drips. That it was best for her if she came to terms with the new her.

The new Lily who had different blood running through her veins, cleaned by machines. The new Lily who had needles stuck into her, pumping metals and vitamins and drugs into her system.

Acceptance.

Acceptance.

She had to accept. She had to take the things inside her, the liquids that they injected, and see them as part of her, not as poison from the outside. She thought of how she'd seen herself when the iron was injected yesterday, a whole lifetime ago it seemed, how she'd felt that she was being made into a new person, only the outline remaining the same.

That was what she had to accept. That she was a new, sick person who needed help, from the outside. Who needed things to go *in*, through tubes and needles.

She could not lock it out.

She rolled up her sleeve and presented her arm to the snake.

"Go on, then," she said. "Bite."

And he looked at her and smiled, showing those needle teeth.

And he did.

28

The teeth sank in, and Lily felt venom, actually felt it, running through her veins up her arms, and she fancied she could see it, too, a sort of green glow, spreading through her. She felt warm and tingly all over.

Something inside her, making her new.

"It'sssss done," said Snake, and his head pulled away. He curled up on the floor, his shape writing a kind of satisfaction against the whiteness of the tiles.

Lily stepped onto the pressure plate again, and again she heard a hiss and a click.

And the second bolt slid open, and all around the door was a bright, thin rectangle of light, uninterrupted by locks.

Lily turned the handle.

The door swung open, just a little.

Beyond it was bright light, the brightest Lily had ever seen; she could make out nothing outside the room because she was so blinded by it.

"This," said Crow, "is where we say goodbye."

Lily turned, startled. The brightness of the light beyond the door echoed against her retinas fuzzily.

Crow and Mouse and Mole sat there, or stood there—how could you really know with things that had four legs or wings? Snake was a spiral next to them, tightly wound.

"No," Lily said. She really was crying now. She wanted to rub her eyes with her sleeve, but she was holding the baby; the baby was getting a little heavy now, actually, even as light as she was.

"Yes," said Mouse.

"Yes," said Mole.

"Yessssss," said Snake.

"It has been an honor to fight by your side!" said Mouse.

"You are brave, for a human," said Crow. "You did not give up. That is something to be proud of." He paused. "Please don't cry. Please."

"We're just manifestations of your unconscious," said Mole. "There's nothing to be sad about."

"No," said Lily. She was thinking of when Mouse had

bit her fake dad's ear, stabbed him with the nail, and he'd yelped. "You're not."

"No," said Crow sadly. "We're not."

For a long moment no one said anything.

"We don't cry," said Crow. "But we would be. If we could. We thank you, Lily Wilson. You saved us too."

Lily smiled at that. She crouched down and hugged them with one arm, holding the baby carefully in the other; they squeezed in and she hugged all of them, a big, feathery, furry, smooth-scaled hug that went on forever and for hardly any time at all, and they were all of them encompassed in the circle of her arm.

Then she let go. And stood, holding her baby sister.

"I imagine you are very pretty," said Mole. "I feel your heart. Your kindness. They warm me inside, like a bellyful of worms."

"Um, thanks," said Lily.

"Wipe away your tears," said Crow. "You have people to speak to. Things to say."

Lily knew that. She would start with apologizing to her parents, for what she'd said the day before, when she'd left the house. "What about you, though?" she said to Crow and the others.

"We won't speak again," he said gently. "But we'll always be there. You will see us, sometimes, maybe. You mustn't weep."

"Oh, is she still crying?" said Mole. "Oh no! Don't cry!"

"It's all right, Mole," said Lily, remembering when Crow pooed on her head, what seemed like forever ago. "I'll use you to wipe away the tears."

"I'd be proud to," said Mole.

And that made Lily cry more. "I was joking, actually," she said between sobs. "I'm holding the baby."

"Yes," said Crow. "Yes, you are."

Lily took a deep breath, imagining that the air was strength, that it would hold her up, like helium holds up a balloon, so she could walk through the door, float through it.

"You have our respect and allegiance, alwayssss," said Snake.

"Thank you," said Lily.

"But now you have to go," said Crow. "Questions are for humans—but knowing when to come and when to go? That is a thing we can do."

"I'll miss you," said Lily.

"We know," they said.

"Look for me in the sky," said Crow.

"Look for me in the earth," said Mole. "Actually, don't. It disturbs the tunnels."

"Look for me under the cupboards," said Mouse. "But don't tell your mum if you see me. She'll buy traps."

"You can look for me if you like," said Snake. "But I'm pretty well camouflaged."

Lily gave a little smile. "I'll always remember you," she said.

"And we will always remember you," they all said together. "Our blessings are upon you." It was oddly formal, that last phrase, the words almost a spell, something to ring the room like it was a bell being struck, and then their voices stopped and the air ceased vibrating.

Lily opened the door wide, light flooding all around her, erasing everything but her silhouette, her and the baby in her arms, and stepped through.

isoriented, Lily blinked a little room into being, with one of those electric folding beds taking up most of it. In the corner was a TV on a swinging frame, hooked to a remote control by a long cable. There was one not-very-comfortable-looking chair, with her dad in it.

In the bed was her mum, sitting up, dressing gown tied.

And by the window—they were high up, looking out over the city, its houses and cars and trees down below—was a doctor. Lily could tell by the woman's white coat and the stethoscope around her neck. Lily wondered if doctors did that deliberately, so you could tell they weren't nurses. They never seemed to use the stethoscopes, in her experience.

" . . . white blood count is totally normal," the doctor was saying. Then she turned to Lily. She frowned very slightly, but then smiled. "Oh, hello."

"Hello," said Lily matter-of-factly, holding her baby sister. This was how it worked, then, with the animals and the magic. People saw something odd, a girl coming through a door that shouldn't be there, then . . . didn't see it. The doctor looked nice: a splash of freckles across her nose, glasses shoved up into messy, curly hair.

"So. Um. No sign of any infection," said the doctor, speaking to Lily's parents again. "Your baby's small, but she's mighty."

Lily thought of Mouse and swallowed.

"I think we can happily discharge you," continued the doctor. "The ear checks and so on have been done, I think? The heel prick?"

"Yes," said Lily's dad.

"Great. And do you have a name yet? There's a registry office right here in the hospital."

Lily's dad looked at Lily's mum, then at Lily.

"No," said Lily's mum, eyes on Lily's. "We'll decide that together."

The doctor nodded. She tapped on her clipboard. "There's also . . . the other tests," she said. She glanced over at Lily.

"She's a perfect donor match. The baby. There was only a twenty percent chance, as you know. So that's excellent."

To Lily's surprise, her dad started to cry. Just, instantly. Just like that. He stood and came over to Lily and the baby. "Really?" he said.

"One hundred percent," said the doctor.

Lily's dad put an arm around her. "Do you want me to take the baby back?" he said. "You've been holding her for a while."

"No, I'm fine," said Lily, which was true.

The doctor was smiling at them, and Lily's mum seemed to be crying now too.

"What is it?" said Lily.

"Well," said her mum. "The thing is that . . . The thing is that the baby might just save your life. When she's a bit older."

"There's a fighting chance, anyway," said the doctor.

"Oh, Lily's a fighter," said her dad. "Aren't you?"

Yes, Lily thought. Yes, she was.

Lily looked down at the baby, and the baby opened her eyes, bigger than seemed possible, dark blue, ringed by long eyelashes, great pools, gazing back at her. Pools that went on forever.

"Only . . . ," said Lily. She was thinking of the locked

room, the pressure plate, how her weight on its own had not been enough. "Only," she repeated, "I think she might already have. Saved my life, that is."

The window was a panel of light. The sun was low, because of the time of year, and there was a haze on the horizon, low down, and the haze was heaven.

30

They didn't have the car, so Granny Squeak came to pick them up. By the time they were actually discharged, it was late afternoon again, and Lily couldn't believe that almost a whole day had somehow gone, like a coin dropped down the side of a sofa.

There were all kinds of different nurses to see, and checks to do, and packages to be given, with pamphlets and diaper samples and things. And Dad had to go buy a baby car seat because, apparently, that was the one thing they hadn't thought of, and Mum had thrown away Lily's because she'd read something about the foam losing its strength over time.

But finally, they were ready to leave.

"Fourteen pounds for an hour's parking!" Granny said as she inserted the little ticket to make the parking lot barrier open.

"Two hours, really," said Lily's dad. "We were getting the baby dressed and all packed up."

"Still," Granny grumbled. Then she glanced back at the baby, and Lily thought she caught the corners of a smile in the rearview mirror. "And when are you going to name the little creature, anyway?"

Lily's mum squeezed Lily's hand in the back of the car. "We're taking our time," she said. "We're doing this together."

"Hmm," said Granny. "So much so that I found an empty guest bed this morning! A little girl hailing a cab to gallivant across the country. I've never heard the likes of it." Dad said it would give Granny a heart attack, female taxi driver or no female taxi driver.

"We'll be talking to her about that, Mum," said Mum.

"Yes, I'm sure," said Granny with a little sniff. "I'm glad she got to you safe and sound, though."

They drove, and as they passed from streets and streetlamps to the open country, the light changed—Lily could feel spring, in the clear white brightness of it hanging in the air, making all the trees pop starkly against the darkening sky. When they got back to the house, the crocuses in the beds out front had opened, a little sea of purple.

"Season's changing," said Granny as she helped carry all the baby things up the front walkway.

"A lot's changing," said Dad, putting his hand on the door handle. Inside, the lights were still burning brightly. "Strange," he said. "I could swear I turned those off." Then he turned the handle and frowned. He pushed against the door. "Won't open," he said in a confused tone.

"We locked it," said Mum.

"I know. But I unlocked it." He held up his key to the Yale lock.

"Oh!" said Lily. She took the rusted old key from her pocket, the one with the long barrel for the old, old lock. She inserted it in the bottom keyhole and turned. The door swung open easily.

Her parents were staring at her. "Where did you find that?" asked her dad. "Looks medieval."

"It's a long story," said Lily.

Granny Squeak walked back to her car. "I'll be off," she said. "Think you need a little family time. I'll bring you a lasagna tomorrow."

"Thanks, Mum," said Mum, and Granny got back in her car, revved the engine noisily, then pulled away.

Lily's parents led the way to the new kitchen, and they all

sat round the big oak table after Dad put the kettle on to make tea. Lily had only recently started drinking it, and she loved how grown up it made her feel, how like one of them, and there was a warm feeling inside her and the tea only made it warmer, when her dad brought it over, sweetened with sugar.

"Don't tell your mum," he usually said. But Mum was focused on the baby right then.

"Wait," said Lily. "I need to check on Buster."

"I left out plenty of food," said Dad.

Yeah, thought Lily. *Not what I'm checking.* "I want to see him anyway," she said.

"Not too close for too long," cautioned her dad automatically.

She went to the utility room, and Buster looked up when she opened the door, panting happily. He trotted over and bent his head to be petted. His eyes were normal now. Maybe they had been before? Maybe he'd only been surprised to find a girl and a mouse entering through the doggie door and hadn't recognized Lily immediately? Maybe she'd even smelled different, because of the yesterday's treatments at the hospital?

It didn't matter, really.

Thank goodness he's friendly again, thought Lily, which

reminded her of Mole; it was the kind of thing Mole would have said.

She went back to the kitchen and her parents.

And the baby.

Lily sat and drank her tea and looked out at the garden, beyond the big glass doors. Late-evening sun shafted down between white clouds, and the sky was the impossible dark blue of the dusk in the early part of the year. A couple of daffodils were out already, pale splashes of yellow against the green.

She remembered, about the tree.

"Um," she said. "About a name. You know I've got the May tree in the churchyard?"

"Yes, darling," said her mum.

"Well. I thought . . . For the baby. Maybe we could plant a cherry tree. In the garden. And we could call her Blossom, and the tree would be for her, and it would flower in the spring, just like her."

Her mum and dad looked at Lily for a long moment. Then they both smiled.

"It's perfect!" said her mum.

"Yes!" said her dad. "I did think we might have been hasty, cutting down the old one."

"And the animals would like it," said Lily, thinking of what Crow had said when they'd first met, about the cherries.

"What?" said her dad.

"The crows—they would like the cherries," said Lily.

Her dad wrinkled his nose. "Yeah, they were always stealing them before they ripened. Maybe we could put up netting."

"You're not putting netting up in my nice garden," said Lily's mum, and Lily took another sip of hot tea, the warmth blooming inside her, and she grinned, because this was home.

"Blossom," said Lily's dad, looking down at the baby, who was in the removable car seat on the floor, sleeping. "Yes. She's a Blossom."

"Welcome home, Blossom," said Lily's mum. Then she blinked. "Oh! Mike. The present."

Lily's dad opened his eyes wide. "On it!" he said. He left the kitchen and came back a minute later with a gift, wrapped in paper with storks on it. "From the baby," he said, handing it to Lily. "From Blossom."

Lily smiled, taking it, and began to unwrap it.

She stopped smiling when she saw what it was.

31

You don't like it?" said Lily's mum.

"No . . . no, it's not that. It's . . . they're . . . lovely."

She looked down. Nestled in a plastic holder was a family of mice, for the big woodland-creature house she had up in her room. A mummy, a daddy, a girl, and a baby—just like them. Dressed in little clothes that you could take off, their bodies made of hard plastic, covered in soft, flocked fur. You could move their arms and legs, put them in the car, sit them at the kitchen table.

There were two problems, though: one was that Lily didn't play with the toy house anymore; she hadn't for years, practically; and the other was that the little mice had hard black eyes, almost coal black, that reminded her of the replacement parents and that made her breathing go fast and shallow.

"Are you okay?" said Dad. "You look pale."

"I'm fine," said Lily. "Just . . . surprised. But thank you. I mean, thank Blossom."

Lily's mum looked stricken. "She needs rest. You need rest, Lily. It was a long night. I've been so . . . I didn't think. It's not long since your dialysis."

Lily realized this was her escape, from having to explain why the mice freaked her out. "Yes," she said. "Yes, I'll go up to bed." She was tired, actually. She hadn't known it until she said it.

"I'll come with you," said Mum. "Don't want you falling down the stairs."

So Mum held her under the arm as she went up, and Lily let herself sink a little, let Mum take a bit of her weight. On the way up the stairs they passed Willo. He hadn't fallen out of her T-shirt in the cellar; he'd fallen on the stairs.

In her hurry, in her haste, Lily must have missed him when she was running downstairs, the dad-thing chasing her. She bent and picked up her stuffed whale.

"Wait, I forgot something downstairs," she said.

"I can't get it for you?" said her mum.

"Not that kind of thing. I'll only be a minute."

"Um, sure," said her mum.

So they went back to the kitchen, Lily carrying her fat toy whale, and Dad was still there, with Blossom. Lily kneeled and put Willo next to her, next to Blossom, in the car seat, the whale filling the space between her little body and the side of the seat, as if it were meant to be there.

"I have a present for her too," she said.

Her parents were looking at her as she straightened back up.

"Are you sure?" said her dad.

"Yes," said Lily. "It's okay. I don't need him anymore."

32

When they came to her bedroom, Lily sat on the bed.

"Do you want anything to eat?" asked Mum. "Shall I bring something up?"

"Um. Yeah, thanks. Anything," said Lily. "No rush."

"All right, darling," said Mum. "Just make sure you rest. If you're asleep, I won't wake you. Do you need a book or anything?"

"No, I'm fine, thanks," said Lily. She felt a flashing pang of guilt. "I'll, um, play with the mice. If I can't sleep."

Her mum smiled, and that only made Lily felt more guilty. Then Mum left the room slowly—Lily could see she must still be sore from the birth. Once she head her mum's footsteps receding down the hall toward the stairs, Lily got straight up from the bed and picked up the mice. She couldn't have them in the house, not with those eyes.

Hard black eyes.

She tiptoed to the baby's room, where the window was still open from when the father-thing had thrown her out of it and then down the rubbish chute, and now she took careful aim and threw the mice out the same way.

The package flew true and hit the inside of the chute before rattling down and landing in the dumpster. At some point tomorrow Lily would have to go down there and get them out, hide them better. But for now they were outside and she was inside, and that was all that counted.

She went back to her bedroom, exhausted, and lay down on her bed, all her clothes still on. From somewhere, she could hear the baby crying. Then her mum was talking about changing diapers, asking her dad for warm water and . . .

She opened her eyes again, and it was full night. There was a plate by her bed, with a sandwich on it. A glass of water next to it. Moonlight shone through her window.

Somewhere far away an owl hooted.

But there was something wrong. What was it?

Then she realized: there was no light, no artificial light. Usually there was a nightlight in the hallway outside her room, plugged into a socket. Usually her parents left the bathroom light on too—there were no streetlights on their road, and it could get very dark.

As it was now.

Lily listened. She couldn't hear anything. Not even her dad's snoring, which was normally loud. Not the baby crying.

She got up, very slowly, and went out onto the landing. Dark. Silent. She crossed the top of the stairs and eased open her parents' door.

They were lying on the bed, very still, their eyes open but looking right up at the ceiling, seeing nothing.

Lily's heart tripped, fell—into an abyss—and she clutched at her breast until it stumbled into beating again. Were they dead? No. Their chests were gently rising and falling.

She moved past the door.

The parent-things stood there, in the moonlight by the window, holding the baby. Lily could tell it was a real baby this time, could tell it was Blossom. They had Blossom. They had taken her from her bedside bassinet and were holding her.

An image floated up in Lily's mind. The horseshoe, the iron horseshoe, the one that had hung above their back door until their back door had disappeared so they could have a big new kitchen, the horseshoe that she had leaned against the paint cans outside.

The horseshoe that she had not hung back up, at the rear of the house.

"Hello again," said the father-thing.

"Time for you to leave for good," said the mother-thing.

33

L ily stood, not a person, but an empty space cut out of the world, hollowed by fear.

She was on her own. She was on her own, and the animals had gone, and that meant . . .

That meant she didn't need them anymore. They'd said that, Crow had said that: if they were there, it meant she needed them. So it followed that if they weren't, she didn't.

Lily looked at the parent-things. The fear was receding now, bleeding away from the edges of her, leaving flesh. Life.

What had they kept saying, the animals?

What you need is inside you.

Lily looked down at her hands.

Hands.

Arms.

Body.

She turned her arms over, looking at them. She thought of the feeling when Snake had bitten her, of something flooding through her. She thought of the father-thing, recoiling from the iron key.

Iron.

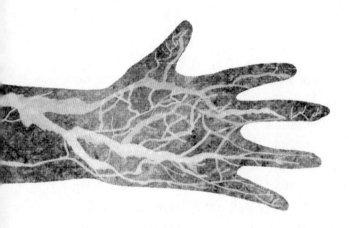

She pictured the doctor, yesterday—only yesterday, though it felt like a hundred years ago—injecting her with a big dose of iron, bigger than most people would ever get from their food, more iron than most people would have in their system at any one time; a massive dose to refill her body's reserves and keep them topped up for weeks.

Iron, she realized with a smile. It was what was inside her. It was the answer; it had always been the answer. It was iron, she had it in her blood, a whole syringe full of it.

She knew it, and everything was clear.

"Why are you smiling?" said the mother-thing. Her voice was deadly cold.

Oh, to have Mole here, with her dim wits and sharp hearing. Crow, with his silly advice, which was sometimes actually useful. Mouse, with his ridiculous bravery. Even Snake.

But Lily was brave enough on her own, she supposed.

"I just . . . ," said Lily. "I don't know. I can't fight any more. I don't want to fight any more. So I give up."

"You . . . ?"

"I give up. I want this to be over. I'm not going to leave, though. I choose to stay. To leave my sickness behind."

"It's not your choice," said the mother-thing.

"Yes, it is. You told me. I can choose to join you. Give you my . . . life force. I can choose to be hugged by you. And . . . I don't know. You breathe your breath into me, and then I'm part of you or something. You said you could take my suffering away."

"Yes. Once you have stopped breathing for yourself," said the father-thing, observing her, head inclined.

"Yes," said Lily. "So do it."

"Do . . . it?"

"Hug me. I'm sick of this body anyway."

The parent-things came away from the window, converged on her. Their eyes glinted in the moonlight. The baby in the mother's arms stirred, just gently, and whimpered. A real baby now. Lily's sister.

"You choose this, of your own volition?" the mother said.

"Yes," said Lily. She was so afraid again now that the world was shrinking and expanding, shrinking and expanding, as if the universe were something that breathed.

"Very well."

Both parents stepped forward.

"Wait," said Lily. "Give her to me first. My sister. When I'm gone . . . then you can do what you want."

The mother-thing frowned, but after a moment she nodded. She handed over the bundled baby, black eyes on Lily all the while, and Lily held her little sister close. She could feel the baby breathing softly, fast asleep.

She laid her in the bassinet, and Blossom sighed, then breathed deep, low down in sleep, peaceful, oblivious to what was happening above her.

The parents approached Lily. The air ticked down a degree as they neared, became colder.

And Lily tensed, despite herself, and they put their arms around her, and then there was a feeling like tightening bands, like two boa constrictors, not that Lily had ever been circled by a boa constrictor, felt it squeezing the life out of her, but that was what was happening. She managed a shallow breath, and then another, and then—

—then no more, and there was just a silvery emptiness inside her, and then not even that, because they were still hugging, still gripping her ever tighter, and it seemed she might be pressed into a new, smaller version of herself, a doll, and it hurt, oh it hurt, and then—

—with a pang, she remembered she'd thrown Blossom's gift down the rubbish chute, she shouldn't have done that, and then—

—then the mother-thing brought her lips to hers, breathing out already, breathing out whatever passed for oxygen inside her. And Lily?

Lily, who had kept her arms out, out like a cross by her sides—

—Lily *hugged back*.

34

Nothing happened, and Lily was struck, right there and then, by the certainty that she was going to die; or rather, not die, but instead become a monster, like them, and never die at all.

Part of being human, Lily was learning, was that you might die at some point; you had to accept it.

But.

But then she felt the parent-things trying to pull away, and she knew it was from the iron in her blood, the iron resonating through her, pumping out of her heart and into her arteries and making a long song all through her, before looping back through her veins.

She held them closer, did not let them go.

Did not let them go.

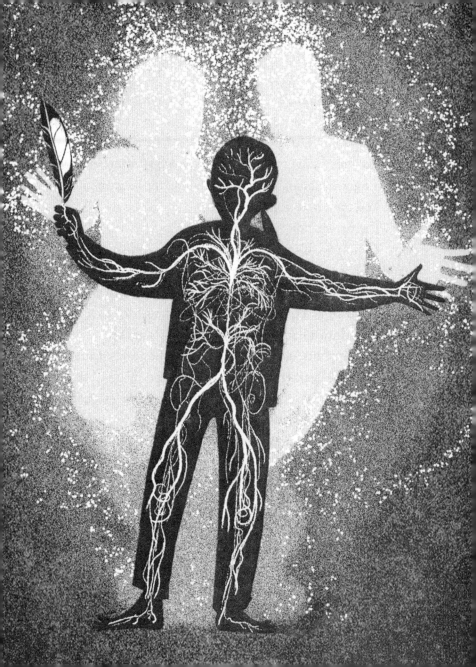

And then:

A soft pop, not even like a balloon, but like a balloon far away, in another garden maybe, and another pop, and all around Lily was sparkling dust, stars, hanging in the air, tiny particles hanging there, an explosion frozen in time, tiny fragments filling the air, then falling to the ground.

And they were gone.

The parent-things were gone.

There was black stuff on the floor, dustlike, sootlike, and then it rose into the air, rose like a special effect, swirling, spiraling, and it twisted upward and sharpened and was sucked, with a sound like a video winding backward, like air being drawn back into lungs, into Lily's pocket.

Lily felt burning hotness in there. She reached in and took out the feather, the feather from the magpie, which was now a kind of pulsating, glowing black, emanating colossal heat, almost burning her hand.

She looked around quickly.

The fireplace. She could almost hear Crow saying it, almost see him pointing to it with his wing. Old things were powerful, after all. Old things such as fireplaces.

Lily dashed over and threw the feather in; it burst instantly into flame, converting itself into glitter-dust that hung a moment there, in the chimney, then shot up it and out of the house.

An image appeared in Lily's mind, an image of a piece of metal bent into a U.

And she knew there was one more thing that she needed to do for this to be over. She listened. Her parents were sleeping soundly, the real ones. The baby, too. Lily went to her and picked her up and held her close against herself.

She wasn't about to leave her little sister unprotected.

35

When Lily came to the bifold doors in the new kitchen extension, she lowered the lever and slid them open, easily, smoothly, all with one hand while the other arm held Blossom.

Outside, she listened. She heard a car engine somewhere far off, a shout from the pub down the road, the squeals of a cat fight or something like it. It was only now that she realized that the whole time, the whole time the parent-things had been around, there had been no sounds coming from outside at all.

She went to the paint tins, gravel crunching underfoot. The baby slept warmly against her, cradled in one arm, stirring only when a cool breeze swept over the grass.

Lily bent and picked up the horseshoe.

Something moved.

Her head snapped up, and she saw them: two shadows on the lawn, where nothing was there to cast them. The shadows glided toward her.

Her heart tightened.

Then they came closer and arced up, over Lily's head, and she could see they were magpies. Two magpies. Two for joy.

The magpies whirled over her head, and as they did so, a feather loosened and fell. It turned softly as it came down to rest on Lily's outstretched palm.

She placed the horseshoe down for a moment and put the feather in her pocket.

A new one, should she ever need it. Two magpies were better than one, after all, as Crow knew.

Stars glimmered in the sky, sparkling starrily, things that were fire and warmth in the dark, that were light, no matter how far away.

She went back inside, the horseshoe in her hand, the feather somehow warm in her pocket. A charm. A talisman. A weapon.

Above the doors there were hooks her mum had put up, and hanging from them were the half-hearted paper-chain decorations Lily had made that year.

She tore them down with her free hand, then looked for somewhere to put the baby. The car seat was still there; her dad must have taken Blossom out to carry her upstairs. Her real dad, safely sleeping upstairs.

Kneeling down, she laid her little sister gently in the seat and buckled her in.

Then she dragged over a chair, stood on it, and hung the horseshoe above the doors. She'd have to explain that to her parents, she guessed. She wasn't sure how. But something would come to her.

Outside the windows, the magpies turned one last time, lofted into the air, and merged with the night.

And just like that, it was over. They were gone, the parent-things, really gone. Lily could just feel it. She looked down at Blossom's face, her long eyelashes, her gently rising and falling throat, and she smiled.

Even though she knew the baby was too young to smile— her parents had forewarned her of that—as Lily stared at Blossom sleeping, she could have sworn her little sister's lips curled up at the edges in return.

She lifted the car seat by its handle and struggled down the hallway with it, then up the stairs. It was heavy and awkward for her to carry. Although she entered her parents' bedroom as quietly as she could, her dad nevertheless rolled over with a huffing sound when she came in, and she could tell they were sleeping normally now. Her real parents were sleeping normally in their bed.

The thought made Lily breath easily for the first time in a long time.

She put down the car seat. Another thing to explain—how it had gotten upstairs. But her parents had been tired—maybe they'd attribute it to that. Very, very slowly, Lily unfastened the strap around Blossom and lifted her sister up, returning her to the bassinet beside her mum.

Eyes closed, still apparently asleep, her mum reached out a hand, touched Blossom, checked she was there, then smiled and rolled to face her. Lily backed away, out of the door.

She crossed the landing and slipped on something, almost fell. The beads from her necklace.

Stooping, she picked them up, picked them up slowly and painstakingly, and threaded them back onto the string. She went down the stairs, getting them all, from the bottom too, where they'd run down and into cracks beneath the wainscoting. She didn't know if she would wear the necklace when it was done—it was mostly for her mum, had been her mum's idea in the first place.

But maybe she would. It would be a way to say: *That was me. I did those things, I went to all those appointments, I changed. I am not the me I was before, I have iron in my veins and in my heart, and that's one of the things that makes me me.*

Or something.

She went back up the stairs and carefully returned the necklace to the bowl. The little night-light on the landing was back on. She walked into her room and saw something that made her breathing stop again.

The family of mice, on her bed. At the foot of it, on top of her owl duvet. The present. She hadn't noticed it there when she'd gotten up.

Her heart hammered in her chest. How were they back here when she'd—

But wait.

One of her parents must have seen them in the garbage bin, right? Or heard her throw them out—the sound of something skittering down the chute?

She picked them up. Beneath them was a note:

Thought you might change your mind.
Know you're a bit old for them, but you
can play with them together, when your
sister's a bit bigger. Dad. XOXO

Lily looked at their eyes. They weren't hard and black anymore; maybe they never had been. They were made of blue felt. She took the mice out of their packaging and stood them on her bedside table, by her mushroom lamp.

The whole family, together.

AFTER THE END

More than a year had passed.

It had been a really good Christmas this time, and now it was spring again. Just last week it had started to be full light when Lily woke for breakfast before school. Birds sang as she got dressed. The skies in the evening were torn and pink, below a vast expanse of electric blue.

No school today, though.

Today she was in the garden. Her dad was doing something to the lawn. Raking up moss or whatever. Lily was wearing her bead necklace. She always wore her beads now. She'd earned these beads.

"This damned mole," her dad said. "We never had moles before the extension."

Lily smiled. There were molehills all over the lawn. It

drove her dad mad. He'd wanted to bring in a pest control person, but Lily had put her foot down—no dead moles—and her mum had agreed.

So mostly Dad just grumbled about it.

Above Lily, the new cherry tree spread its pink-flowered branches. They'd bought it last summer. It wasn't Blossom's tree. Blossom's tree had been planted as a tiny seedling in the churchyard; Granny Squeak had been there, along with cousins and friends.

But Blossom's tree wouldn't grow cherries for seven to ten years, that was what Dad said, so Lily had pleaded for a tree for their garden too, a mature one, and that was what grew above her now, dappling the light on the lawn with its branches.

Lily sat on the grass and let sunlight play on her eyelids.

Meanwhile, Blossom herself played beneath her name-sake. More than one year old now, she was waddling around, often falling on her bottom but getting straight back up again, standing from a crouch all in one go, like one of those little toys with elastic between the joints, where you press a button underneath and they snap upright.

She walked a distance, turned, tottered back to Lily.

"Lala," she said. That was what she called Lily. "Lala, bubba."

"Okay, Blossom," said Lily.

She raised the bottle of bubbles, took out the wand, and blew. Bubbles streamed out toward Blossom, some of them floating up into the air and over the cherry tree, some of them racing down the lawn.

From inside, Lily heard Mum laughing at something on the radio.

Around Lily and Blossom bubbles floated, popping softly, leaving little glistening particles, stars, hanging in the air after they disappeared.

Blossom giggled, chasing them.

"Keep her away from the steps, Lily," called Dad.

"Of course," said Lily. "Over here, Blossom."

Blossom waddled back toward her.

"Lala! Lala!"

Such a good girl she was, such a good girl. Lily thought her heart might burst with love.

But not with anything worse than that. She still had drips and injections and she didn't run away from them anymore, but she was going to be better one day, no longer having to go to the hospital. That was because there was going to be a part of her sister in her one day, her parents had explained—the surgeons were going to take some of

Blossom and put it in her, a part her baby sister didn't need. When she was big enough.

Lily was going to get her transplant.

But Lily thought there was something her parents didn't quite understand: there was already a part of her sister in her.

A sudden gust of wind blew, and Blossom's downy hair stood on end as she laughed. Somewhere a crow called: *caw, caw, caw*. The branches of the cherry tree shivered in the wind, and then there were blossoms falling all around Lily and her sister, little stars and sunbursts and fractals, flowers of it, frilled, petals of white and pink, between the low, low heaven and the earth.

"Oh!" said Dad.

"What?" said Lily.

"Just then," said Dad, "in the wind. Blossom looked just like you, at the same age."

Lily looked at Blossom, surprised. Then she smiled. Because her little sister was perfect.

Acknowledgments

My deep thanks go, as always, to Hannah Lake, as well as to Katherine Rundell, Sarah Crossan, Imogen Russell Williams, Rachel Denwood, Lucy Rogers, Lucy Pearse, and Krista Vitola for wise counsel at various stages of the writing of this small but tricky book.

And now to the book itself—not just the words of it. I am profoundly grateful to Emily Gravett for illustrations so beautiful that seeing them was the highlight of my writing life so far, and to David McDougall for a design more thoughtful and exquisite than I could have imagined.

Publishing is alchemy, I've always thought—and everyone at S&S, in both the US and the UK, has brought transmuting magic to this story.